Middle School Millionaires

by Roderick J. Robison

Copyright © 2013 by Roderick J. Robison

Library of Congress Card Number: 2013902921

ISBN-13: 978-1481892803
ISBN-10: 1481892800

Also by Roderick J. Robison

The Principal's Son
The Christmas Tin

For Mom, who always supported and encouraged the businesses of my youth

And for Larry Strasner, my childhood business partner

Chapter 1

The Garbage Business

September 20, 1989

Here we go, thought Kirk Atwill.

It was two minutes before the dismissal bell on Wednesday afternoon. Mrs. Harlowe had just picked up a stack of papers from her desk. The lady was always trying to fit in one more homework assignment before the end of class. She walked toward Kirk's desk—the first one in the first row.

"Take one and pass the rest along," she instructed.

"Yes ma'am."

Kirk sighed. Today of all days, he did *not* need an additional homework assignment. Kirk removed the top sheet and passed the stack down the row. Then he glanced down at it to see what he was in for…But it wasn't homework! It was the schedule for the After School Program.

"Be sure to give these to your parents," Mrs. Harlowe instructed. "The After School Program starts up next week for those who are interested."

Kirk crammed the schedule into his notebook—the wastebasket was too far away to discard it.

Brriiiiinngg!

"See everyone tomorrow," shouted Mrs. Harlowe.

Kirk was the first one out the door. He was always the first to leave. That was the good thing about sitting in the first seat of the first row. He was at his locker pulling his jacket on a few moments later when Bud Dentin approached.

"There's a street hockey game down at the tennis courts this afternoon," Bud said. "See you there?"

"Sorry," Kirk responded. "Can't do it today. I've got business to take care of."

"Okay, catch you later."

"See ya, Bud."

Kirk strung his knapsack over his left shoulder, headed down the hallway, and exited Horace Clovis Middle School through the double-door main entryway. Outside, the September air was crisp, the sky clear. The first hints of fall could be seen in the leaves of the maple trees that bordered the schoolyard, where a group of eighth-graders had just started a game of flag football.

"Hey Atwill," one of them yelled. "We need another player."

"Can't do it today," shouted Kirk. "Business waits."

It wasn't that Kirk didn't like sports. He did. But he had a business to run. Kirk was in the *garbage* business. And today, Wednesday, was his busiest day of the week. Wednesday was trash collection day in the town of Belton, Michigan.

That morning, while his classmates were still fast asleep,

Kirk was pulling barrels of rubbish to the curb in front of his customers' homes. This afternoon he would pull the empty barrels back from the curb and return them to his customers' garages and storage sheds. He had started the business the year before, when an elderly woman on his snow shovelling route asked him what he would charge to haul her rubbish to the curb on trash day. After he started to haul her rubbish to the curb each week, some other residents saw him in action and inquired about his rates. And his business grew from there.

Kirk had always been entrepreneurial. His knack for business first became apparent back in preschool. Kirk was helping his aunt sell apple cider in a booth at the harvest fair at his cousin's elementary school. The going rate was 25 cents a cup.

Business was slow at first; Kirk soon became bored and turned his attention to the coins in the cash box. Though he was very young, Kirk knew the value of the coins. His dad was a coin collector; Kirk had always been fascinated with his dad's coin collection. He'd often helped his father sort coins and separate them into piles. He knew that nickels were greater than pennies, and that dimes were greater than nickels, and so on. He knew too that dollar bills were more valuable than any of the coins…and he noticed that there were *no* dollar bills in the cash box.

His aunt was in the back of the booth pulling a gallon of cider from the cooler, when a woman and her two children approached.

"How much for a cup of cider?" she asked.

Kirk looked up at her and smiled. "A dollar."

The lady said, "Three cups please." She handed him three dollars, and just like that, Kirk had quadrupled the price of the cider. After that, each customer paid the new going rate of a dollar per cup. The cider booth had never been so profitable.

There were other early displays of Kirk's knack for business too. In second grade, he was the top seller for the PTO fundraiser. He sold seventy-seven candy bars—more than twice as much as the kid who took second place. And there was the time in third grade when his cousin and her friends had a lemonade stand. The lemonade stand was located on a side street.

There wasn't much business at first. But then Kirk came along and assessed the situation. He quickly noted a crew of painters working on the neighbor's house across the street. He brought each worker a free sample cup of lemonade. Half an hour later the entire crew showed up at the lemonade stand. They bought two cups a piece and returned later on for refills.

Kirk repeated the process with a landscaping crew at work down the street. And then he posted signs along neighboring streets. Business picked up dramatically. It was a banner day; his cousin and her friends sold six gallons of lemonade—a neighborhood record.

Kirk made his way across the school grounds, headed down Main Street, and crossed over onto Pleasant Street. There was a spring to his step. Trash day was also pay day. It was the day his customers left payment envelopes for him.

But what made this afternoon even better was the prospect

of *new* business. New business meant more money. Just down the street, he noted a moving truck in front of the Jenkins old house. The Jenkins moved out the month before.

The new owner, the Johnson family—soon to be his new customer—would be there this afternoon. The movers had told him so that morning when he stopped by on his way to school. Taking on a new customer was an exciting thing.

Kirk calculated the extra money in his head as he walked toward the house: five dollars a week to pull the rubbish. And there might be more too. The driveway and walks would need to be shoveled come winter. That would bring in ten dollars per storm easy. If these people went on vacation, he'd offer to watch their house and bring in the mail. The price: a dollar a day. If they had a dog, he'd offer to walk it. If they had a bird, he'd clean the cage. Everything had a price.

Yes sir, taking on a new customer was an exciting thing all right. And securing this account was a sure thing. Kirk lived on the street, just six houses away. And he had a lot of references in the neighborhood. In fact, he pulled the rubbish for the people next door.

Kirk ambled up the front walkway and up the stairs to the front porch. Then he rang the doorbell and removed a business card from his jacket pocket. A few seconds later the door opened. A middle-aged woman stepped out.

"Hi ma'am. I'm Kirk Atwill. I live just down the street. I just wanted to welcome you to the neighborhood, and let you know about my services in case I can be of any help."

Smooth. Kirk handed her a business card.

"I pull rubbish to the curb on trash day. And I rake leaves and shovel snow too," Kirk informed her. "My prices are very reasonable."

The woman glanced at the card…and handed it back to him with a sympathetic look.

"I'm sorry, young man. I'm sure you're a hard worker and all, but another boy stopped by a little while before you. I've already hired him to help us out in these areas."

Aaaargh!

Kirk didn't need to be told the boy's name. He knew it all too well. Ever since Tommy Hartwell had moved to town last spring, he'd been a thorn in Kirk's side. Tommy Hartwell had copied Kirk's business. The kid's mother was a real estate agent. It seemed that lately, Tommy was always one step ahead, getting the inside scoop on new homeowners in the neighborhood. Heck, the kid's mother was probably pitching business for him, putting a good word in for the kid. It just wasn't fair. Tommy Hartwell had almost as many customers as he did now! And Kirk had been at it a lot longer.

Is he helping you with *everything*? Kirk asked.

"Yes, I'm afraid so," the woman replied. "Thank you very much anyhow. It was nice to meet you Kirk. If things don't work out I'll give you a call."

"Yes ma'am." Kirk sighed as he turned and walked down the stairs and headed home. He knew she'd never call…but what he didn't know was that his afternoon was about to get worse. A lot worse.

Chapter 2
The Competition

Kirk's mother was in the kitchen unloading groceries when he stopped home to grab a snack. "Why the sad face?" she asked.

"I'm loosing business to Tommy Hartwell," Kirk complained. "He's invading my territory!"

"Well, I'm sure there's enough business around here for both of you," Mrs. Atwill assured. "Here, these will cheer you up." She handed Kirk a can of cashews. His favorite snack.

"Thanks Mom," he said, taking a handful of cashews. He placed his backpack on the kitchen table.

"Any notices from school?" his mother asked, rummaging through his backpack. Even though he was in eighth grade now, his mother still went through his backpack each day.

"No, nothing important," Kirk replied, heading upstairs to his room.

His mom was perusing the schedule for the clubs in the After School Program when Kirk stepped back into the kitchen a few minutes later, clad in his work clothes—torn jeans, work boots, and a faded flannel shirt.

"I'm going to be volunteering at the library on Mondays,"

his mother announced. "And where I'm not going to be here that day, the After School Program might be just the ticket. Why don't you look over the clubs and pick one that interests you?"

"I'm in eighth grade now," Kirk protested. "I'm old e-nough to stay in the house by myself."

"No, you're not honey. Maybe next year."

"Awe, come on Mom."

"There's no negotiation on this one," his mother stated. "I just don't feel right about you being here alone. And your father will surely feel the same."

Kirk sighed. He'd never been interested in the after school clubs in elementary school, and he certainly wasn't interested in them now, in middle school. He had better things to do.

Kirk reluctantly grabbed the schedule and sat down at the kitchen table. Then he perused the Monday afternoon offerings. The POTTERY CLUB was of no interest. Neither was ARTS & CRAFTS. And BATON TWIRLING was out; YOGA held no appeal. BEGINNING CHESS seemed too basic. The only thing that looked re-motely interesting was the YOUNG ENTRE-PRENEURS CLUB. Kirk studied the course description:

For the entrepreneurial-minded student. Learn how to successfully start and run a small business. Students will learn the basic fund-amentals and strategies needed to successfully operate a small business.

"Okay," Kirk said. "If I have to choose one, I'll go with the YOUNG ENTREPRENEURS CLUB."

"Great. Sounds like that one's right up your alley."

Maybe I'll pick up something to give me an edge over Tommy Hartwell.

Kirk grabbed his work gloves and another handful of cashews.

"Bye Mom."

"I hope you have a profitable afternoon," his mother replied. "Dinner's at six."

"Thanks Mom."

Kirk's mood brightened after he collected the first few payment envelopes. Money had a way of making things better. But then he noticed the kid heading up the sidewalk toward him... Tommy Hartwell.

Kirk scowled as Tommy neared; Tommy smirked. They gave each other menacing sideways glances as they passed each other. Neither spoke.

Mr. Craigmoore was the last customer on Kirk's route. The man was one of those fussy, tough-to-please customers. The type of guy that was always trying to whittle the price down to save a buck. Last winter, he'd tried to negotiate with Kirk to cut his shoveling price in half—after the walk had been shoveled. And during the heat of summer, he was the only customer that didn't opt to pay Kirk an extra dollar to swab the stink out of his barrels.

The man did have one good trait though. He promptly left a payment envelope taped to his front door each Wednesday...until today.

Kirk noticed that the envelope was missing right away. He climbed the front steps and knocked on the door. Mr. Craigmoore opened the door, an envelope in his hand. "This will be your final payment," the man said, matter-of-factly.

Kirk was dumbfounded. "Oh?"

"Yes. I've found someone else to pull my rubbish," stated Mr. Craigmore. "A boy that will pull my rubbish for fifty cents a week less than you."

Once again, Kirk didn't need to hear the boy's name. He knew instantly who had taken business from him.

"But I always pulled your rubbish on time," Kirk protested. "In rain and snow. I've always been there."

"Sorry son. Money talks."

First this kid gets the jump on new business. And now he's taking away my existing business!

If something wasn't done quickly, Tommy Hartwell would soon have *all* of Kirk's business.

*****

Two new customers in one day. That was a record for Tommy. He was all smiles as he walked over to visit his mother at her real estate office that afternoon. Things were going well. Very well. He was catching up with Kirk Atwill.

Tommy had envied Kirk's business since moving to Belton six months ago. Kirk's customers were loyal. That was for sure. The kid was reliable, had a good reputation. Tommy had talked to most of Kirk's customers. Tried to win their business. But the only customer he'd been able to sway so far was Mr. Craigmoore—and that was no easy feat. He'd had to lower his price. Nevertheless, he had gained a new customer. And his business was growing.

His mother was at her desk viewing Belton's single family home listings on her computer when Tommy arrived.

"Hey, Mom."

"Oh, hi kiddo," she responded, looking up from her computer. How's business today?"

"Great! I'm going to be pulling the Johnson's rubbish over on Pleasant Street. Thanks for putting in the good word!"

"No problemo."

"I got another account today, too."

"Sounds like you're on a roll!"

"Today, anyhow. Kirk Atwill still has a lot more customers than I do." Tommy grabbed an apple from the fruit bowl on the desk.

"I'd say you're doing just fine," his mother replied. "Building a business takes time."

"I guess so," Tommy said. "Have any more homes sold?"

"None yet, but I'll keep you posted."

"Thanks Mom. See you later."

"See you tonight…Oh, and Tommy?"

"Yes Mom."

"Don't forget to bring *our* rubbish barrels back to the

garage this afternoon."

"*Yes Mom.*"

All in all, things were looking good for Tommy Hartwell. Kirk's loss had been his gain that afternoon; he was pleased with the way things were going. And he enjoyed a very deep and satisfying sleep that night.

Two streets away, Kirk Atwill tossed and turned in his bed. Kirk didn't find sleep that night. It wasn't until the early morning hours that he finally drifted off.

Chapter 3

The Young Entrepreneurs Club

Three students were already seated in Room 102 when Kirk arrived for the first YOUNG ENTREPRENEURS CLUB meeting on Monday afternoon: Albert Jensen, Sarah Maxwell and Laura Tompkins. Kirk walked across the room to the last row and took a seat. It was a nice change to be able to sit in the last row for once. He didn't know the other three students. He wondered if he were in the right room. Kirk reached into his backpack to check the room number on the schedule…and then Tommy Hartwell walked into the room. Now there was no question he was in the right room.

I should have figured he'd sign up for this club.

Kirk narrowed his eyes at his competitor. Tommy did the same when he saw Kirk. He took a seat in the first row. Then the teacher, Mr. Hardwick, entered the room.

"Welcome!" boomed Mr. Hardwick. The man was an eighth grade math teacher who supplemented his income as an instructor for the YOUNG ENTREPRENEURS CLUB. He was also an entrepreneur himself. The man owned a laundromat, a small mail order service, and a painting business, which he operated during the summer months.

Mr. Hardwick was one of those teachers who made learning fun. And he was known for starting each class with a *teaser*. Today was no exception.

"Okay, who's good in math?" he asked. All five students looked at each other. When nobody volunteered, Kirk raised his hand. Math was his strongest subject. Always had been.

"Excellent, we have a volunteer," Mr. Hardwick said with enthusiasm. "What's your name, young man?"

"Kirk Atwill."

"Very good then, Kirk. You have two choices: you can receive ten thousand dollars, *or* you can receive a penny and have it double in value every day for a month. Which one would you choose?"

"Um…Ten thousand dollars," Kirk said.

Mr. Hardwick shook his head no. "Anybody else want to give it a shot?"

Tommy Hartwell's hand shot up. "The second one. I'd take the penny and have it double every day for a month."

"Correct!"

Tommy glanced over at Kirk and grinned.

"Ten thousand dollars is a lot of money for sure," stated Mr. Hardwick. "But a penny that doubles in value daily over the course of the course of a month will give you a lot more—more than a *million dollars* in fact. Let that be a lesson." All eyes were on the teacher now.

"So, here we are," Mr. Hardwick continued. "School is over for the day. Your classmates are out playing sports, or doing whatever it is kids your age do with in their free time these days. And the five of you are here…which leads me to believe that all of you have an interest in business. Well, you've made a fine choice!"

"Perhaps you know someone who owns a small business: a parent, an older sibling, a cousin, an aunt or uncle maybe," Mr. Hardwick continued. "In fact, I suspect some of *you* may already have a small business of some sort. Am I right? How about it? Does anybody here already have a small business? Raise your hand if you do."

Five hands shot into the air.

"Splendid! We're off to a great start. Now, let's take a little poll and see what kind of business each of you has. We'll start with you young man," Mr. Hardwick said, gesturing to Albert Jensen. "Tell us your name and what kind of business you're in."

Albert cleared his throat. "My name is Albert Jensen. I operate a lemonade stand during baseball games down at the town field in the summer," Albert proudly replied. "My lemonade is fresh-squeezed. And I use crushed ice."

"Very good, Albert. I'm sure your lemonade is quite tasty. Many successful entrepreneurs started out with lemonade stands. Now, who's next?"

Sarah Maxwell's hand shot up.

"Okay, go. Name and business please."

"I'm Sarah Maxwell, and I'm in the baking business. I sell cookies door-to-door. Five different flavors: oatmeal, peanut butter, sugar, molasses, and my favorite—coconut almond chip."

"Mmm. And I'm sure they're delicious."

"I'm in the baking the baking business too," blurted Laura Tompkins. "I make birthday cakes. Special order birthday cakes. Oh, and my name is Laura Tompkins."

"Very good, Laura, I'm sure your cakes are equally delicious. Let's see. So far, everyone's in the food or beverage business. Do we have any other types of businesses?"

Kirk raised his hand. "I'm Kirk Atwill. I'm in the garbage business."

Mr. Hardwick's eyebrows arched. "The *garbage* business? Please expand."

"I take out people's rubbish on trash day. I pull their barrels to the curb in the morning, and bring them back in the afternoon after they're emptied by the town's rubbish hauler."

"Hmmm…interesting," remarked Mr. Hardwick. "That's a new one on me. Very enterprising."

He turned his attention to Tommy. "And what business are you in?"

"I'm in the garbage business too," Tommy answered.

"Yeah, he copied me!" Kirk accused. It wasn't Kirk's nature to be so forthcoming but he couldn't help it. The words just seemed to come out on their own.

"It's a free country!" Tommy shot back.

"Aaah…*Competition*," remarked Mr. Hardwick. "Very good! A little friendly competition can be a good thing. We'll be discussing competition in the days ahead. You two will want to pay close attention," he said with a wink.

Kirk and Tommy glared at each other.

"All of you are in luck!" declared Mr. Hardwick. Kirk and Tommy shifted their eyes back to the teacher. "We're going to be covering some things that will help each of you succeed in your business. But first things first." He turned around and faced the white board. Mr. Hardwick was a large man. Nobody saw what he wrote on the board until he stepped aside a few moments later and turned to face the class.

Income – Expenses = Profit

"Profit!" Mr. Hardwick exclaimed. "The primary goal of many small businesses is to generate a profit. And to make a profit, your business must earn income. And the income must be greater than your expenses. It's that simple."

Kirk was already subtracting his expenses from his income. Tommy was busy doing the same thing across the room.

"Okay," Hardwick said. "Today we're going to focus on something that can help enterprising small business owners generate profit. In a word: *advertising.*"

Mr. Hardwick went over to his desk and removed a stack of magazines from the bottom drawer. There were many different publications: *Boys' Life, Sports Illustrated Kids, Girls' World,*

National Geographic Kids, Cricket, Time, Family Fun, Newsweek, and a number of others. He handed a few magazines to each student and said, "Glance through these and look for advertisements. When you find one, raise your hand and share it with the class."

All five students flipped through their magazines. Sarah Maxwell was the first to raise her hand. "Found one," she shouted.

"Thank you, Miss Maxwell. Please hold it up for everyone to see."

Sarah stood up. She held up a *Girls' World* magazine and flipped to a page with a transistor radio advertisement. "Excellent. Good example," said Mr. Hardwick. "This is what is referred to as a display ad. A full page display ad that is. Thank you Miss Maxwell."

"I found one," shouted Laura Tomkins." She held up a *Sports Illustrated Kids Magazine* with a half page advertisement. The advertisement was for candy.

"Very good. Another great example of a display ad. Now, let's see if we can locate a classified ad. Classified ads are much smaller and far less expensive than display ads. They're usually located in the back of magazines; they generally don't have pictures."

Everyone flipped to the back of their magazine.

"Got one," said Albert Jensen. He held up an issue of *Boys' Life*. And he showed everyone a small advertisement for water balloon launchers.

"Good show! That's a classified ad all right," acknowledged Mr. Hardwick.

Tommy Hartwell raised his hand next.

"Yes, Mr. Hartwell?"

"These ads look good and everything, but they look pretty expensive, too. At least the ones in my magazine are. The classified ads alone cost two dollars a word. I could never afford that."

Kirk had the same thought. He almost nodded in agreement. If anyone else had said it, he would have.

"I couldn't afford to advertise in my magazines either," Sarah Maxwell chimed in.

"Same here," said Albert Jensen. "My business is only seasonal."

"Now we're talking," said Mr. Hardwick. "Yes indeed. And this brings us to the second part of today's discussion on advertising. Part two if you will. Many small start-up businesses can't afford to pay for expensive magazine ads, as you have so kindly pointed out. But there is another, far less expensive type of advertising: flyers."

Mr. Hardwick went back to his desk and pulled a stack of flyers from a drawer. All of the flyers were from local businesses. "Take a look at these," he said, distributing them among the five students. "You might just get some ideas for your own business."

There were all kinds of flyers. Each advertised a sale or promotion of some sort. Belton Pizza had a buy-one-get-one-free offer. Bright White Dental offered 50% off the first cleaning for new clients. A dry cleaner offered to clean every fifth shirt for free.

"Sometimes, the best way to make money is to give it away," Mr. Hardwick chuckled. "Special offers and incentives can help attract new customers."

Of course! Kirk thought. *Why didn't I think of that?* Advertising was just the edge he needed to compete with Tommy Hartwell. He could hardly wait for class to end so he could get started. He didn't have to wait long.

"My how time flies when we're talking business," Mr. Hardwick concluded. "That's all for today folks. See you again next week."

Chapter 4

You Lose Some. You Win Some.

Kirk bolted to his room as soon as he got home.

"My, aren't we in a hurry," his mother said as he breezed by. "What's the rush?"

"Business stuff," Kirk shouted.

"Don't forget about your homework."

"I *won't*, Mom."

Kirk went into his father's home office and took a seat in his swivel chair. Then he turned on his father's word processor. It wasn't exactly the most updated model, but it would do. He got down to business. An hour later, after experimenting with fonts, layouts, and wording, he came to the realization that flyers weren't all that easy to make. There was more to it than met the eye.

He went through a dozen drafts, tossing each one into the wastebasket, before being pulled away to dinner. After a few more failed attempts after dinner though, he finally came up with a simple flyer that seemed to work:

Kirk's Trash Service

Rubbish barrels hauled to the curb on trash day.

&

Lawn mowing, snow shovelling and pet sitting.

555-555-1916

His father was finishing up breakfast at the kitchen table when Kirk ambled into the kitchen the next morning—an hour earlier than usual.

"How come you're up so early, sport? It's only Tuesday. Trash day isn't until tomorrow."

"I have some business to take care of this morning," Kirk answered, grabbing his backpack and a cereal bar. "See you, Dad."

"Bye son. Go get 'em."

BERNSTEIN'S PLACE was Belton's busiest neighborhood convenience store. It was Kirk's first stop. There was a bulletin board on the back wall. Mr. Bernstein had put the bulletin board there to allow local businesses to advertise their products or services. It was a win-win situation. Area businesses got to advertise for free. And customers had to walk by shelves of impulse goods, magazines, and other items to reach the bulletin board.

Kirk removed a flyer from his backpack, then grabbed four tacks from his jacket pocket. He tacked the flyer to an area on the right side of the board, nestled among business cards and flyers promoting area businesses: painting contractors, mortgage brokers, real estate agents, cleaning companies, and landscapers. Then he stepped back and glanced at it. The crisp, bold print stood out on the bright white copy paper. It looked good. Better than good; it was sure to attract some attention.

The next stop was BELTON WASH-A-MATIC, the town's only laundromat. It was just down the street. There was a bulletin board there too. Kirk posted a flyer on it, amid the other advertisements.

After that, he stopped by the town common. There, on the wall next to the bus stop, was the biggest bulletin board of all. It was the most widely read too. Many local businesses used it. Kirk tacked his last flyer on the board and headed to school, thinking of all the new business he'd obtain. Tommy Hartwell would no longer be a concern; Kirk would soon have more business than he could handle.

The school day ticked by. Classes dragged on, each one seemingly longer than the one before. Even PE took forever. Kirk heard little of the classroom discussions; his mind was on business. He was anxious to see how many phone calls he received from the flyers. When the dismissal bell finally rang, he wasted no time. Kirk was out of the building before most kids had reached their lockers. He checked the answering machine as soon as he got home ...but it wasn't blinking. Nobody had called.

Kirk stayed close to the phone that afternoon. But it still didn't ring. Suppertime came, and still nobody called. Kirk kept an ear out that night too, but by the time he turned in for the night, the phone still hadn't rung. Nor did it ring the following day or the day after that. Not for business anyway. There were just the usual calls from his grandmother and friends of the family.

Kirk began to wonder about the flyers. Maybe someone had placed their flyer over his. Maybe his flyers had been torn down, or perhaps they fell down. He decided to get up early the next morning to check them out.

As he neared the bulletin board at BERNSTEIN'S PLACE, Kirk could see that his flyer was still up. This brought some relief…until he noticed the new flyer right next to his. This flyer really stuck out—it was printed in fancy type on vibrant yellow paper with a red border around the edge. It was more professional than Kirk's. He froze when he read the bold lettering on the first line:

Tommy's Rubbish Removal

Tommy offered a free week of service for new customers. Kirk's face reddened.

It was the same thing at BELTON WASH-A-MATIC: Tommy's vibrant flyer was right next to his. And of course, Tommy had placed a flyer on the bulletin board at the town common as well. No wonder Kirk hadn't received any calls. He wanted to yell at Tommy Hartwell. Had their paths crossed on the way to school that morning, he would have.

Kirk's anger intensified as the day wore on. But sometimes, what goes around comes around. And just when it seems things are at their worst, something good happens. In Kirk's case, that something was a phone call that came just after dinner. His parents listened as he took the call in the kitchen.

"Hello?...Yes, this is Kirk…Oh?…Really?…Yes, I'd be glad to…I'll start next Wednesday…Okay. See you then. Bye."

There was a stunned expression on Kirk's face as he hung up.

"Sounded like good news," his father observed.

"It was," Kirk replied. "I just landed a new customer. The Johnson's—the new family on Pleasant Street."

"I thought Tommy Hartwell got that account," Mrs. Atwill remarked.

"He did. But he lost it."

"Oh?"

"Apparently, Tommy didn't pull the barrels back to their garage by the time Mr. Johnson came home from work on Wednesday. The guy ended up taking them in himself."

Kirk enjoyed a deep sleep that night. The same couldn't be said for Tommy Hartwell.

Chapter 5
An Unlikely Partnership

The month of October was an interesting one for the students in the YOUNG ENTREPRENEURS CLUB. There were four meetings that month, and each one proved to be a learning experience. Kirk and Tommy listened intently, trying to pick up tricks to gain a competitive edge over the other. It was as if they were in a race to see who could win the most new business.

When Mr. Hardwick explained the benefits of "branching out and expanding your market," they went further out into new neighborhoods, knocked on doors in hope of gaining new customers.

When Mr. Hardwick informed the class that "customers can be a good source for referrals for new business," Kirk and Tommy talked with their customers to see if they had friends, neighbors, or relatives that might be interested in their services. And when Mr. Hardwick talked about the benefits of "add-on selling," they went back to their customers once more and reminded them about the additional services they could provide, such as lawn mowing, raking leaves, snow shoveling, and pet sitting.

By the end of October, the rivalry between the two

of them was as fierce as ever. The two despised one another. They avoided each other in the hallways at school, took different routes home from school so they wouldn't have to see each other. They had no idea that their lives were about to become intertwined. If they had, they both surely would have dropped out of the YOUNG ENTREPRENEURS CLUB at the end of October.

*****

The second to last YOUNG ENTREPRENEURS CLUB meeting fell on the first Monday of November. The topic of discussion: partnerships.

"Partnerships," Mr. Hardwick began, "can be a wonderful thing. Partnerships have many benefits. If you have a business partner, you don't need to worry about your business when you're on vacation. Your partner can handle the show while you're gone. In a partnership, you can take on additional work that you might not have been able to handle on your own. There are other benefits too. Partners can brainstorm new ideas together. And they can pool their resources. The list goes on and on. Yes sir, there are many benefits to partnerships."

"Of course, for a partnership to be successful," Mr. Hardwick explained, "both partners need to contribute equal time and energy. And partners have to be compatible in order to work well together." He gave Kirk and Tommy a wink.

"A good partnership is like an engine with well-oiled gears. A bad partnership on the other hand...Well. There are those too. Suffice it to say, you need to find the right business partner for things to work."

Mr. Hardwick rambled on about the *pros* and *cons* of partnerships for the better part of the meeting. And then, toward the end, he made a surprising announcement: "You have a homework assignment."

This brought a number of moans. A rumble of disapproval swept through the room. This was an after school club after all. There wasn't supposed to be homework. None of the clubs had homework. Everyone knew that. The students already had more than enough homework in their regular classes.

"I know, I know," Mr. Hardwick consoled. "Don't worry. It's not the type of homework you're accustomed to. This will be a *fun* assignment. And it will be due at our final meeting, one week from today. "

"For this assignment," he said, "you're going to pair up with a partner to form a fictitious business. This business should be different than the one you currently have. Choose something new. Choose a business that you and your partner can research together."

Mr. Hardwick handed out a sheet of guidelines. "You and your partner are going to write a one-page report on your business, a mini-business plan if you will, using these guidelines. And most importantly, there must be a reason *why* your customers will choose to do business with you instead of the competition. Anyone can start a business, but to be successful, you need to find a reason for people to use your service or product over that of the competition. You need an edge. Use your imagination people, and let's see what you come up with. Surprise me. Come prepared to give a brief oral presentation on your business."

Laura and Sarah had already paired up before Mr. Hardwick had finished. And Albert Jensen was out sick, which meant...

"Kirk and Tommy, you two will be teaming up together."

Kirk and Tommy traded glances. Neither had any intention of talking to the other, let alone working with him.

"I look forward to hearing about your new businesses next Monday," said Mr. Hardwick. "A week is a lot of time, but I recommend that you start earlier rather than later. That's it for today. See you next week."

Outside the classroom, Kirk headed in one direction, Tommy the opposite. It wasn't looking good.

****

Kirk's mother was backing the Chevrolet out of the driveway when he got home. "I'm heading to the supermar-ket," she said. "Want to come along?"

"Sure Mom. Be right back."

Kirk tossed his backpack in the front seat and bolted off to the garage. A minute later he returned and hopped in the front seat with a small bag full of bottles and cans. The returnable type. That was the other way Kirk made his money: by returning bottles and cans. Thanks to Michigan's bottle bill, he made 10¢ for each re-turnable bottle and can he returned. All he had to do was deposit them into the reverse vending machines at the supermarket. There was one machine for bottles, and one machine for aluminum cans. Each machine printed up a receipt afterward. He simply took the receipts to the customer service desk and exchanged them for cash. It was that easy. Kirk had been collecting bottles and cans and bringing them there for years.

Kirk felt fortunate to live in Michigan. Michigan had one of the highest paying bottle bills in the country. Most of the other bottle bill states paid only 5¢ per container. And many states had no bottle bill at all. To Kirk's way of thinking, the only drawback to the state's bottle bill—if you could call it a drawback—was that there were hardly ever any bottles or cans to be found along Belton's streets and neighborhoods.

Though there was talk of implementing one, the town didn't have a recycling program. Only trash was collected at the curb each week. Some of Kirk's customers set bottles and cans aside for him on trash day. And he scrounged through the rubbish barrels at the town fields for bottles and cans too. Lately though, the barrels held only trash. Kirk speculated that Tommy Hartwell was the culprit. There seemed to be fewer bottles and cans around since the kid moved to town.

"So, how was school today?" his mother asked, during the drive to the supermarket.

"It was good… up until the YOUNG ENTREPRENEURS CLUB."

Mrs. Atwill furrowed her brow. "Oh? I thought you liked that club."

"I did— until Mr. Hardwick gave us homework this afternoon."

"Well, the way you seem to enjoy that class, I'm sure it can't be *that* bad."

"It's worse than bad—I got paired up with Tommy Hartwell to do a project."

"Aaah. That explains it. Working with the competition, eh? So, what's the project?"

"We're supposed to come up with an idea for a new business and write a report about it."

"Sounds like a fun assignment if you ask me. For both of you. What type of business did you two come up with?"

"We haven't."

"Did you brainstorm some ideas?"

"We're not exactly on speaking terms, Mom. We don't talk."

"No?"

"Nope. I hate him. And he hates me."

"Hmm. Well, it looks like you two are going to have to start *talking* soon. I'm sure you'll work it out."

I doubt it.

When they arrived at the supermarket, Kirk fed the bottles and cans into the reverse vending machines. There were seventeen bottles and five cans in all. The receipts amounted to two dollars and twenty cents. It wasn't much, but it added up after a while.

Kirk cashed in the receipts at the customer service desk, then caught up with his mother. His thoughts wondered back to the YOUNG ENTREPRENEURS CLUB meeting as he walked down the aisle, tossing cereal, breakfast bars, and macaroni & cheese into the shopping cart. He found himself trying to think of a business for the homework assignment. But then he stopped. Tommy Hartwell hadn't given it a thought for all he knew. Why should he?

*****

Three days passed. Kirk and Tommy hadn't talked to each other. As usual, they avoided each other at school; it was as if they were both holding out, willing the other to talk first. Both had a stubborn streak; neither of them was going to give in first. But then came Friday.

Mrs. Englemeir was at her desk scribbling a note when Kirk walked into Room 212, for math, just before second period. He was the first student to arrive, and he promptly took his seat. Mrs. Englemeir looked up at him and smiled, then continued writing. She was scheduled for lunch duty that afternoon, but there was a conflict in her schedule. She had a parent-teacher conference booked for that time. The note she was writing was to another eighth grade teacher, Mr. Boutner. She was asking him to cover her lunch duty. Teachers covered lunch duty for one another now and then.

The other kids entered the room and took their seats. A few moments later, just after the second period bell, Mrs. Englemeir stopped writing. She glanced over at Kirk and held out the note.

"Could you bring this to Mr. Boutner? she asked him. "He is in the teacher's lounge."

"Sure." Kirk always enjoyed the opportunity to get out of class for a while. What student didn't? That was another benefit of sitting in the first seat in the first row—whenever a teacher needed something dropped off or delivered, they asked the kid closest to the door. Kirk took the note and headed out into the hall.

The teacher's lounge was on the second floor, just down the hall from the music room. When Kirk reached the teacher's lounge a few minutes later, the door was slightly ajar. He cautiously peeked in. Mr. Boutner was sitting on a couch along the left wall, his feet propped up on a coffee table. The man was drinking a can of soda and perusing a magazine. In the right corner of the room was a soda vending machine. On the floor beside it rested an old metal trash can.

Kirk knocked gently on the door. "Um, excuse me…Mr. Boutner?"

The man looked up from his magazine. "Yes?"

"Mrs. Englemeir asked me to give this to you, sir." Kirk held out the note.

"Bring it over."

Kirk had never before set foot in the teacher's lounge. No student had. The teacher's lounge was forbidden territory, strictly off limits to the student populace. Kirk slowly stepped into the room. He handed the note to the man. Mr. Boutner accepted it, read it, and then jotted something down on it. Then, just before he handed the note back to Kirk, the guy raised the can of soda to his lips, finished it in one gulp—and tossed the can into the rubbish barrel... And that's when the idea came to Kirk.

"Thanks Mr. Boutner!"

"No trouble, young man." The teacher had no idea what he was being thanked *for*.

Kirk didn't learn anything in math that morning. Nor did he learn anything in social studies. His mind was racing. And for the first time ever, he found himself actually looking forward to seeing Tommy Hartwell.

Tommy was at his usual table when Kirk entered the cafeteria at lunchtime. The two of them always sat at different tables, far apart. Tommy raised his eyebrows when he saw Kirk headed his way.

"Mind if I sit down?" Kirk asked him.

Tommy shrugged. "Suit yourself."

Kirk placed his tray on the table and took a seat across from Tommy.

"What's up?" questioned Tommy, a curious tone in his voice.

"I've got an idea for the homework assignment, for a business... unless you have something."

"I don't," said Tommy. "What's your idea?"

Kirk took a gulp of milk. Then he told Tommy his idea.

Tommy nodded between bites. He listened intently as Kirk talked. The business Kirk described was a simple one. It involved placing a recycling barrel beside the soda machine in the teacher's lounge—a barrel for ten-cent returnable cans. The teachers could deposit their cans in the recycling barrel, rather than the trash barrel. Kirk and Tommy would collect the cans and bring them to the redemption machine at the supermarket. They would make ten cents per can. All they had to do was empty the barrel and return the cans to the supermarket.

"I like it!" said Tommy. "It will be a good report…But we could actually do it. We could put a recycling barrel *in* the teacher's lounge. And make a little money."

Kirk paused for a moment. "I hadn't considered actually going through with it," he said. "But it would make for a stronger report. Do you think we'd be allowed to do it?"

"I don't know. Maybe we could ask Mr. Putnam, the janitor. "

"Good idea."

"Let's catch up with him after last bell," said Tommy, as the period drew to a close. "See you then...partner."

Anyone observing the conversation would never have guessed that the two of them had been arch rivals just minutes before.

*****

Mr. Putnam removed his hat and scratched his head. "You want to put a second trash barrel in the teacher's lounge?"

"A *recycling barrel*," Kirk clarified. "For a school project."

"We're in the YOUNG ENTREPRENEURS CLUB," Tommy explained.

Mr. Putnam raised his eyebrows. "Well, that's a new one on me boys. But if you two want to spend your money on a new barrel for the teacher's lounge, I don't know why anyone would want to stop you. While you're at it, you might want to consider placing one in the cafeteria as well."

"The cafeteria?"

"Yes. A vending company is going to be putting a drink vending machine in the cafeteria next week."

"A *drink vending machine*?"

"That's right," said Mr. Putnam. "For carbonated drinks: flavored mineral water and fruit juice. Word just came down from the superintendent's office. The machines are going to be placed in all of the school cafeterias."

"Thanks Mr. Putnam!"

"No problem, boys. You'd be doing me a favor, actually. Meet me here tomorrow morning around eight o'clock. I'll open the teacher's lounge for you. And then we'll go to the cafeteria."

"You got it. See you then, Mr. Putnam."

"So, I guess we need to get two barrels, pronto," Tommy declared on the way home that afternoon.

"You got that," said Kirk. "Jacob's Hardware Store sells barrels. They open at 7:30 tomorrow morning. We could stop there and get them first thing. Maybe stop by the diner and get a cup of coffee for Mr. Putnam too."

"Sounds like a plan," said Tommy. "I'll make up a few signs for the barrels."

"Great… But there's something we haven't worked out yet."

"What's that?"

"Mr. Hardwick said we need to come up with a reason *why* people would want do business with our company instead of the competition. We need something that will give us an edge on the competition."

"Hmmm… That's right," Tommy acknowledged. "Tell you what. You came up with the idea for the business. Let me see what I can come up with for this."

"Deal. See you in the morning…partner."

Chapter 6

The Business Plan

Mr. Hardwick's words echoed in Tommy's mind when he sat down at his parents' word processor later that afternoon to make signs for the barrels. *There must be a reason why your customers will choose to do business with you instead of the competition.* That was the real challenge. It was like Mr. Hardwick said. Anyone could start a business. But to be successful, you needed an edge over the competition. So far, he hadn't come up with anything. "Tommy, time for dinner," his mother called. "And tell your father too."

"Sure Mom."

His father was in his study, just down the hall. Mr. Hartwell was a Certified Public Accountant. The man was reviewing a set of documents when Tommy entered the room.

"Dinner's ready, Dad."

"…Okay son…Be right there."

"What are you working on?"

"…I'm auditing the books for a nonprofit organization," his dad replied, without looking up from the paperwork on his desk.

"A *nonprofit organization*?" Tommy questioned. He'd never heard the term. Mr. Hardwick had always stressed how important it was for businesses to *make* a profit. Profit. Profit.

Profit. That's what it was all about. Why would any company not want to make a profit?

"….Yes…A not-for-profit business," his father confirmed.

"Why would a business want to be nonprofit?" Tommy asked. "I thought making a profit was what it was all about."

Mr. Hartwell hesitated, then slowly looked up from his paperwork. "There are several reasons," he explained. "Nonprofits don't have to pay income taxes. And nonprofit companies are charged a lower postal rate for mailings too. They're often charitable organizations. Organizations that help people in need."

Just then, something Mr. Hardwick had said came back to Tommy: *Sometimes, the best way to make money is to give it away*. This got Tommy thinking. The gears in his business mind were starting to click.

"What about a *half profit* company?" he asked his father. "Is there such thing as a half profit company?"

Mr. Hartwell's eyebrows raised; he looked up from the paperwork once again. "I can't say I've ever come across a half profit business before," he admitted.

"But do you think it would be possible for someone to set up a *half profit* business?" Tommy inquired.

"I don't know what sense it would make, but sure. A business could be set up as half profit, I suppose. Such a business might not enjoy the same benefits as an actual nonprofit business, but there's no law against it that I know of—"

"Thanks Dad!"

Kirk was just coming down the stairs for dinner when the phone rang. Mrs. Atwill picked up.

"Hello…Yes…Okay. I'll get him."

She whispered to Kirk. "It's your competitor—Tommy Hartwell."

"Thanks Mom. I'll take it in the den." Kirk picked up the phone a few seconds later.

"Hey Tommy."

"I figured it out. I know how we can get our customers to choose us over the competition."

"How's that?"

"We're going to give our profits away."

Kirk wasn't sure he heard right. "Give away our profits?"

"Yep. That's right," declared Tommy. "We're going to give our profits away."

The kid actually sounded serious. Until now, Kirk had always figured Tommy for a savvy businessperson.

"Are you crazy? That's the best you could come up with?"

"Let me rephrase," Tommy said. "We're not going to give away *all* of our profits—just half of `em."

"I don't get it," said Kirk. "Why would we give half of our profits away?"

"Okay. It's like this. The teachers in the teacher's lounge have been depositing their empty soda cans in the old barrel beside the soda vending machine. That old barrel is our competition. The way I see it, the teachers can keep discarding their cans in that old barrel, like they've been doing—or they can deposit them in the new recycling barrel we'll place beside the soda machine. They'll have two choices now. We need to give them a reason to toss their cans into our barrel instead of the other one. To do this, we'll place a sign on the barrel stating that half of the profits from the cans deposited in the barrel will be donated to charity. By depositing cans in our barrel, the teachers will be doing a good thing. And we'll be doing a good thing too. It's a win-win situation."

"And the same holds true for the barrel we'll put in the cafeteria. Kids will have the choice of depositing their cans and bottles in the regular barrels—or ours. We need to give them a reason to choose ours. I figure it's like Mr. Hardwick said, 'Sometimes the best way to make money is to give it away.'"

"Aaah… I'm with you now. Great idea!"

Tommy smiled. "Now, I guess we just need to come up with a name for the business."

"I think you already have."

"Huh?"

"*Half Profit Recycling*," Kirk grinned.

"Works for me."

"Me too. Okay, I'll see you at the hardware store tomorrow morning at seven-thirty," said Kirk.

"See you then, partner."

*****

"Good morning, boys. What brings you in so early on this

fine day?" asked Mr. Jacob.

"Barrels," said Kirk. "We need two of `em."

"All of the barrels are at the back of the store," the proprietor told them, gesturing out back with a sweep of his hand.

Kirk and Tommy made their way to the back of the store. There were half a dozen different types of barrels. But the least expensive was $10.99.

"Pretty expensive for a school project," Tommy declared.

"For sure," Kirk agreed. Neither of them had ever *bought* a barrel before. Their customers always had their own.

"How much money do you have on you?" Tommy asked.

"Four bucks."

"I've got three-fifty," Tommy replied. "Guess we're out of luck."

They were heading toward the front door when Mr. Jacob said, "Find what you where looking for boys?"

"We did… But they're too expensive," Kirk replied, his tone sullen.

"Just what are looking to do with these barrels?" the old proprietor asked.

"School project."

"Hmmm… Give me a minute, boys." Kirk and Tommy glanced at each other and shrugged as Mr. Jacob disappeared into a room at the back of the store. A few moments later, he returned with two dark green barrels with matching lids. They were dusty, but after he wiped them down with a rag, they appeared new.

"A landlord ordered twenty-five of these last spring. I set

'em aside for him, but the guy never picked 'em up. They're discontinued now. And I can't return 'em. Tell you what. I'll give you these two barrels if you fellas come back here at closing time tonight at six o'clock and sweep the floor."

"Deal! Thanks Mr. Jacob."

"My pleasure boys. See you at six."

"See you then, Mr. Jacob."

"I hope so."

Kirk and Tommy each picked up a barrel and exited the hardware store. Next stop was the coffee shop.

It felt strange entering Horace Clovis Middle School before first bell; it was a first for both Kirk and Tommy. There was an emptiness to the place without the murmur of student voices and slamming lockers. The two of them felt better when they heard Mr. Putnam whistling. They found him in front of the teacher's lounge.

"Hey, Mr. Putnam."

"Oh, hi there fellas. Got your barrels, I see."

"Yes sir," said Kirk.

"This is for you, Mr. Putnam." Tommy handed the janitor a cup of coffee.

"Well, thanks boys." A slow grin took shape on the janitor's face as he pried the cover off and took a long sip.

"Aaaah...just the way I like it: cream & sugar, heavy on the cream. Much obliged. Well, we might as well get to work, eh?"

Kirk and Tommy followed the man into the teacher's

lounge. Even with Mr. Putnam there, it still seemed like stepping into forbidden territory.

"Might as well place the barrel right here beside the other one," Mr. Putnam advised, pointing to the old barrel beside the soda machine.

"Will do," said Kirk. He placed the barrel while Tommy opened his backpack and removed one of the signs he had made the night before. It read:

10¢ Deposit Cans & Bottles Only Please

Thank You

Barrel provided by Half Profit Recycling.

Half of the profits from the containers deposited here go to charity.

Tommy taped the sign to the front of the barrel. Then the three of them stepped back and admired the barrel. The recycling barrel and its matching cover stood out in sharp contrast next to the older one. Tommy's sign was very professional looking. But something was still needed.

"Hold on," said Mr. Putnam. He removed a pocketknife from the sheath on his belt and walked over to the barrel. Then he cut a round opening in the lid, just big enough to drop a can through. "That's better."

"Thanks Mr. Putnam!"

"No trouble, boys. Why don't you leave the other barrel with me? I'll take it down to the cafeteria on Monday and put it by the new drink machine."

"That'd be great!" Tommy taped a sign on the second barrel. Then he handed the barrel to the custodian.

"Well guys, I've got to run," said Mr. Putnam. "I'll be here next Saturday morning from 8-12, if you want to stop by to empty the barrels."

"That would be great. Thanks again for all your help, Mr. Putnam."

"Glad to help out."

Next Saturday couldn't come soon enough!

Chapter 7
Easy Money

The new drink vending machine stood out in sharp contrast against the cafeteria's west wall. It was a source of great excitement during lunch period on Monday. A group of students were gathered around the new vending machine when Kirk and Tommy ambled into the lunchroom at the beginning of eighth grade lunch period. Some of the larger kids were elbowing their way to the front of the crowd.

The new drink vending machine was candy apple red. It was six-feet tall. The machine offered six different carbonated drinks: Very Berry, Grape, Strawberry-Banana, Lemonade, Limeade, and Raspberry-Lime.

Kirk and Tommy made their way into the crowd. As they neared the machine, they were quick to note that the cans were the ten-cent deposit type. This was good. Then they noted that Mr. Putnam had already placed the Half Profit Recycling barrel beside the machine. Off to a good start.

Edging closer, they casually peered through the opening in the barrel's lid. It was still empty as far as they could tell. But the lunch period had only just begun. Tommy and Kirk waited their turn in line. When it was his turn, Kirk deposited fifty cents. He purchased a Limeade; Tommy bought a Very Berry.

At the lunch table, they were like two detectives on stake-out; their eyes never drifted from the barrel. Ten minutes later, a student across the cafeteria got up to empty his lunch tray. Atop his tray was a can from the drink vending machine. They anxiously watched as he walked toward the machine and the recycling barrel ….only to see the kid pass by the barrel and empty the contents on his tray, including the can, into one of the rubbish barrels by the cafeteria's entrance.

Then a girl stood up nearby. There was an empty beverage can on her tray too. Once again, Kirk and Tommy observed. But she bypassed the new recycling barrel as well, deposited the can into one of the regular disposal barrels. The next kid did the same thing.

"I think we need to set an example," said Tommy.

He stood up and cut across the lunchroom, holding his tray before him, an empty Very Berry can clearly visible for all to see. As Tommy neared the Half Profit Recycling barrel, he slowed. Then, he stopped in front of it. He pretended to take notice of it. And he slowly read the sign. Then he backed up a few steps. And in one fluent motion, he lifted the can from the tray, and tossed it into the opening in the barrel's lid with a deft hook shot. He made a game of it.

Kirk followed his lead. He made his way over to the barrel. He too pretended to study the barrel. Then he held an empty can high up over the opening in the barrel's lid. He dropped it in.

"Two points!" Kirk yelled.

The stage was set. The two of them walked over toward

the disposal barrels to empty their trays. Then they returned to the table and watched.

The next kid got up…and dropped a can into the recycling barrel. Tommy and Kirk nodded. Another student got up and did the same. As did the one behind him. Things were beginning to shape up.

"Easy money," said Tommy, his face creasing in a smile.

"That it is," Kirk agreed.

*****

The spirit was festive at the start of the final YOUNG ENTREPRENEURS CLUB meeting at 3:30 that afternoon. Mr. Hardwick had set up a small table with drinks and snacks in the back of the room.

"First things first," he said. "First we're going to hear a-bout your businesses. Then we'll eat. Let's see. Laura and Sarah, you're up first."

The two girls walked to the front of the classroom.

"We chose a homemade soap business for our project," Laura began. "The name of our company is L&S Specialty Soaps—"

"It should have been S&L Specialty Soaps," Sarah inter-rupted. "I think it sounds better. But to be fair, we tossed a coin to see whose initial would be first. And Laura won." From her tone, it was a sore subject.

"It's only right," blurted Laura. "*L* comes before *S* in the alphabet. L&S sounds better!"

"Okay, okay girls," Hardwick cut in. "Glad you two worked out the naming of your business. Indeed, choosing a name for a business can sometimes be a challenging thing. Please continue."

"All right," said Laura. "We found a soap-making recipe in a book at the library. And we decided we'd add some ingredients of our own: herbs and spices. This would give our soap a unique scent. We'd sell the soap at flea markets and craft fairs."

"My mother works at a salon," Sarah added. "The salon would sell some of our soap, too. We'd give them a commission."

"Splendid girls. Sounds like a fun business. One question though: "Why would people want to buy your soap instead of soap sold by the competition?"

"Our soap would be environmentally friendly," said Laura, "since it would be made with all natural ingredients. Our soap wouldn't harm the environment the way some other soaps do."

"People could feel good about using our soap," Sarah put in.

"Very good," praised Hardwick. "Did you actually make some soap?"

Sarah and Laura looked at each other. "No, we didn't have the ingredients," Laura replied.

"A job well done, girls. You may take a seat. Okay, Kirk and Tommy, you're up."

Kirk and Tommy moved to the front of the room and stood before the class as the girls took their seats.

"Um, we chose an environmentally-friendly business too," said Kirk. "A recycling business. The name of the business is Half Profit Recycling. Tommy and I noticed that the school recycles paper, but not cans and bottles. Teachers in the teacher's lounge have been throwing away soda cans that could be recycled—ten-cent deposit cans that could be returned for a refund. So we figured the teacher's lounge could use a recycling barrel."

Mr. Hardwick nodded.

"And now there is a need for a recycling barrel in the cafeteria too because of the new drink vending machine," Tommy put in. "Our business is a simple one. It involves two recycling barrels: one in the teacher's lounge; one in the cafeteria. These barrels are for returnable cans only—the 10¢ deposit type."

"Interesting," said Mr. Hardwick. "But what makes you so sure people will deposit cans in these barrels instead of the regular barrels?"

"We put some thought into that," Kirk responded. "We're giving half of the profits from each barrel to charity. It was Tommy's idea, actually. We think most people would like to help contribute to charity if given the chance."

"And recycling is good for the environment, too," Tommy interjected.

"Very enterprising," remarked Mr. Hardwick. "I think that business model just might work."

"Actually, it does," said Kirk, with a sheepish grin.

"Pardon me?"

"It works," Kirk confirmed. "We put one barrel in the

teacher's lounge and another one in the cafeteria."

"You don't say!?" exclaimed Mr. Hardwick. "You boys certainly put your time in on this project. Very impressive! A job well done."

"Thanks Mr. Hardwick."

"Okay everyone, we're almost done. But before we conclude and move on to the refreshment table, I'd like to leave you with some final words of wisdom…Sometimes, you just have to go with an idea and give it a try. All the research in the world won't do you much good if you don't take action—like Kirk and Tommy did," Mr. Hardwick said with a wink.

"If you've done your homework and have a sound business plan, that's all well and good. But if you don't act on it, it's of little value. Bill Gates didn't get to where he is today by not taking action. Now, let's dig in. Refreshments everyone!"

Kirk and Tommy joined the others at the refreshment table. They had good reason to celebrate. They had each learned some things that would help them in their rubbish removal business. And their project was a success. They might even make a little money before they removed the barrels. Everything could have ended right there. But it didn't.

Chapter 8

The Right Place At The Right Time

As Superintendent of Belton Public Schools, Burt Stackner made it a habit to periodically visit each school in the district. On the schedule for Tuesday morning was Horace Clovis Middle School.

When he arrived at Horace Clovis Middle School Tuesday morning he found everything in order. The brass kick plates on the entry doors were freshly buffed; the hallway floors gleamed. The grounds were spotless. The front office was impeccable; papers were neatly stacked, documents were properly filed.

Principal Byron Philbrick had put the word out about the superintendent's visit, of course. Just like he always did. And he would likely take all of the credit for the school's pristine condition, the same way he took credit for other people's ideas. Last month, when Mr. Putnam told him about an energy conservation idea that could shave ten per cent off the school's electric bill, it somehow became *his* idea. And when the school secretary came up with the idea for a fundraiser to raise money for a seventh grade field trip, it became *his* fundraiser. It was just the man's nature. He couldn't really help it. His father had been the same way.

Principal Philbrick was seated behind his desk, dressed in

his best suit, when the superintendent knocked on his door.

"G-good morning sir," Philbrick greeted. He got up and extended his clammy right hand. Small beads of perspiration glistened on his forehead. These visits with the superintendent put him on edge.

"Good morning, Byron," said the superintendent, shaking the principal's hand.

"Get you a cup of coffee sir?"

"No thanks. Already had one," the superintendent replied, discretely wiping his hand on his suit pocket. "I guess we should get started."

"Yes sir."

The two of them spent fifteen minutes walking the school's hallways and grounds. Along the way they discussed bussing issues, capital improvements and the upcoming Parent Night. Later that morning they monitored a few classes, and talked with some of the faculty. They concluded the visit in the cafeteria, just before noon.

The superintendent took immediate notice of the cafeteria's new drink vending machine. He nodded approvingly. "Gives the students a little more variety," he said. The superintendent had worked closely with the school committee on the vending machine project. A number of vendors had been evaluated during the selection process.

Then he glanced down and saw the shiny new recycling barrel beside the drink vending machine. He seemed to recall seeing one in the teacher's lounge as well.

"Byron, it's great to see you've implemented a recycling program here at Horace Clovis," he praised. "Good work! You've set a fine example here."

Philbrick was dumbfounded. "...Thank you sir...Yes. We're proud of our recycling program here at Horace Clovis," he sputtered. The truth was he hadn't even been aware of the recycling barrel. Nor had he noted the one in the teacher's lounge.

"Recycling is the right thing to do," said the superintendent. "The other schools in the district could benefit from a recycling program like this too. Byron, I'd like you to call my secretary and give her the number for this Half Profit Recycling outfit."

"Yes sir. I'd be glad to."

"You're doing a fine job here, Byron. Keep up the good work."

"Thank you, sir."

*****

If anybody knew about the recycling barrel and this so-called Half Profit Recycling company, it would be the janitor. Philbrick found Mr. Putnam down in the boiler room just minutes after the superintendent left.

"Mr. Putnam! Are you responsible for bringing the recycling company in?! The Half Profit Recycling outfit?"

Mr. Putnam turned around, hesitantly ... "Uh... yeah... I

guess you might say that. Is there problem?"

"No. On the contrary, the superintendent was impressed with their operation. Liked their barrels. He wants them in the other schools too."

"You don't say?"

"He was most pleased. I need to get their phone number to his secretary, pronto. Do you have it?"

"Uh…I don't actually have the number on me."

"Well, can you *get* it?"

"Yes… I'll plan to get it for you."

"Very good! I'll expect it first thing in the morning."

What ever you say. "Uh, yes sir."

Mr. Putnam didn't know who was in for the bigger surprise: Kirk and Tommy—or the principal.

*****

Kirk and Tommy were just finishing their lunch when Mr. Putnam approached their table. "Boys, we've got a problem," the janitor said, wrinkling his forehead. "We need to talk. Can you meet me in the boiler room in five minutes?"

Kirk and Tommy exchanged glances and shrugged. "Sure. See you there, Mr. Putnam."

So this was it. The end of the road. It was obvious that their "project" had come to an end. Time to pull the barrels and take the cans to the reverse vending machines at the supermarket to cash out. Principal Philbrick or one of the teachers must have caught on to the fact that the recycling barrels belonged to them. It was good while it lasted.

They made it to boiler room in just less than five minutes.

"We had a visit from the superintendent today," Mr. Putnam informed them." He wants to talk to you."

Kirk and Tommy gulped.

"…No kidding?"

"I kid you not," said the janitor.

"Is it about the recycling barrels?" Tommy inquired.

Mr. Putnam nodded. "That's my understanding. Sounds like he wants recycling barrels at the other schools too."

"Wow! Does the superintendent know that it's *our* business?" Tommy asked. "Does he know that Kirk and I are behind Half Profit Recycling?"

"Not that I'm aware of."

"And Principal Philbrick doesn't know either?" Kirk inquired.

"Nope. And I wasn't about to tell him. That's your business, as I see it."

"So what's the *problem* you were referring to?" Tommy asked.

"The problem is Principal Philbrick wants the phone number for Half Profit Recycling. He wants me to get him the number first thing tomorrow morning so he can pass it along to the superintendent…*Is* there a phone number?"

"Yes," said Tommy. "We'll have the number for you to-morrow morning. Before school."

"We will?" questioned Kirk.

"No sweat. Trust me."

"…Okay," said Kirk. "Thanks Mr. Putnam. See you in the morning."

"Glad to be of help boys. Oh—one more thing. We're go-ing to need another barrel in the cafeteria. The one in there now is filling up fast."

Kirk and Tommy glanced at each other and grinned.

"We'll take care of it, Mr. Putnam."

Just then the fifth period bell rang.

"Let's get together after school," said Tommy.

"Definitely. Want to come over my place?"

"Sounds good. I'll meet you at your locker after last bell."

"See ya then."

The two of them talked nonstop on the way to Kirk's house. Placing barrels in each of Belton's schools would be a massive undertaking for two eighth-graders who didn't drive. But Kirk and Tommy weren't your average eighth-graders; they were wired differently than their peers. The two of them lived and breathed business…and they were about to find out if they had what it took.

But first they needed a phone—and a phone number. They couldn't give their home phone number; that wouldn't be pro-fessional. They'd be dead in the water before they started. What they needed was a business phone.

"I've been after my parents for a while to let me get a second phone line so I could use it for business," Tommy said. "The phone company has a special promotion where you can get an additional phone number for $9.99 a month. I'm pretty sure my folks would let me get it if I said I was going to pay for it."

"Excellent! We'll go fifty-fifty on it."

"All right. I'll talk to my folks tonight. One more thing—we'll need an answering machine."

"I've got that covered," said Kirk. "My parents just bought a new answering machine—an updated model with more options. The old one still works fine. We can use that. And we've got an extra phone, too. We can pick them up at my place this afternoon."

"Great. And I guess we'll need to pay Mr. Jacob another visit soon too."

"Most definitely," Kirk agreed. "I think we're going to be doing a lot of sweeping."

Chapter 9

The First Call

"Check it out," said Tommy.

It was ten minutes before first bell the following morning. Kirk was on the front stairs outside the school; Tommy had just met up with him. He removed a small tape recorder from his jacket pocket and pushed the play button. Kirk listened.

Hello. You have reached Half Profit Recycling. We're away from the phone right now, but your call is important to us. Please leave your name and number and a brief message. We'll be sure to get back to you as soon as possible. Thanks for calling Half Profit Recycling.

"That's the message on our answering machine," said Tommy.

"Wow! Sounds like a real business," said Kirk."

"We are a *real* business."

"Who recorded the message?" Kirk wanted to know. The woman's voice sounded very professional.

"My sister, Jenna. She's in high school."

"Fooled me."

"Yeah, she's pretty smooth all right. Oh, good news. The phone company is installing the second phone line this afternoon. And we have a phone number."

"Okay," said Kirk. "Let's find Mr. Putnam and give him the number. What is the number by the way?"

"555-555-5699."

"I like it. Not too hard to remember."

They found Mr. Putnam in the science wing. And things started to fall into place. They gave him the number and he passed it along to the principal, who immediately called it in to the super-intendent's secretary. The superintendent called Half Profit Recy-cling the following day and left a message.

Tommy's heart pounded when he heard the message on the answering machine after school that day. He went over to Kirk's house to give his partner the news. Kirk was at the kitchen table eating a peanut butter and banana sandwich when Tommy arrived.

"Eat fast. The superintendent called. Left a message."

"Wow! That didn't take long."

"You got that. We ought to get right back to him."

It was decided that Tommy would make the call; he had a slightly deeper voice than Kirk. There was a phone in the kitchen. Tommy picked up the receiver, took a deep breath and dialed the superintendent's number. "Um, Superintendent Stackner, please."

"And whom may I ask is calling?" inquired the secretary.

"...Uh...This is Thomas at Half Profit Recycling... returning his call."

"Oh yes, he told me you'd be calling. Superintendent Stackner had to step into a meeting. He updated me though. He said he was over at Horace Clovis Middle School yesterday, and saw your barrels. He would like to get them placed at the other schools too. There are two elementary schools and the high school, in addition to Horace Clovis Middle School. Can you manage that?"

"Not a problem," Tommy replied in the deepest voice he could muster. "We can take care of it this Saturday."

"Very good. I'll inform the superintendent. Do you need directions to the schools?"

"No, we're—er, familiar with them."

"Very well then. I don't want to tell you your business, but I'm guessing you'll want to place more barrels at the high school. In addition to the teacher's lounge and the cafeteria there, you'd be well advised to place a barrel outside the boys and girls locker rooms. Each locker room has a drink vending machine. I'll contact the schools and notify the janitors to let you in Saturday morning. The janitors work from 8-12 on Saturdays. Do you think you'll be able to place all of the barrels during that time?"

"Yes ma'am, that won't be a problem. We'll plan to empty the barrels each Saturday morning between 8:00-12:00, starting next week, if that works," said Tommy.

"That will be fine. Just give me a call if you run into any trouble."

"Will do. And thanks for choosing Half Profit Recycling. Bye now."

Tommy gave Kirk the thumbs up. "We're in business."

"Yeah baby!"

"We're going to need a lot more barrels," Tommy suddenly realized.

"Let's go see Mr. Jacob—and get ready for some serious sweeping."

"Let's go."

Already, their partnership was shaping up nicely. The two of them complemented each other. Kirk was more conservative, whereas Tommy was more of a risk taker. A business needed some of both traits to be successful.

"Okay," said Kirk, on the way home the following afternoon. "One thing we didn't talk about. How are we going to transport the barrels to the schools on Saturday morning? We can't exactly carry them on our bikes."

"I've got that figured out," declared Tommy. "My sister drives. I'll con her—er, ask her to help us out. I'll work something out with her."

"Excellent! But what about the following Saturdays when we empty the barrels? Think she'll be able to drive us then too?"

Tommy frowned. "Knowing my sister, we'll be doing good to get her to help us out *once*."

"So how *are* we going to get to the schools to empty the barrels and collect all the cans?"

"Good question. Let's talk about it over food. All this brainstorming is making me hungry."

"Same here."

When they reached the Atwill residence, they each grabbed an apple and a handful of left over Halloween candy from the bowl on the kitchen table. "We'll be out in the shed," Kirk called to his mother. Tommy followed his business partner out the kitchen door and across the back yard to the garden shed.

The shed had served as a fort for Kirk and his friends growing up; there was no tree in the yard for a tree fort. The shed was a simple structure with a small door at the front. There was a single-pane window on each side of the door. Below each window was a box with red carnations that Mrs. Atwill had planted.

Inside the shed, a workbench lined the far wall. Garden tools hung neatly from nails on the right wall; perched in the left corner was a lawnmower. Kirk's bike was leaning against it. The only furniture consisted of two stools from the clubhouse days. They each pulled up a stool and sat down.

"So, we're all set for this Saturday thanks to your sister," said Kirk, taking a bite from his apple.

"But we really need to think about next Saturday and the ones that follow," said Tommy. "We're going to need transportation."

Kirk glanced over at his bike. Tommy did too. "You thinking what I'm thinking?"

Tommy nodded. "Pedal power."

"Yep."

"… You think we can cover all the schools in a day?" Tommy asked.

Kirk took another bite from his apple and thought for a

moment. "I don't think making it *to* the schools will be a problem. But transporting the cans *from* the schools might be. Would be tough to carry them in bags over the handlebars. Maybe we could jerry rig some sort of cart or wagon to tow behind our bikes."

"That just might work," declared Tommy. "In fact, I think it will. But there's another dilemma too. Where are we going to return all of the cans for a refund? I usually bring mine to the reverse vending machines at the supermarket."

"Same here," said Kirk. "But it's too far across town. It would take us forever to get there. Not to mention the time it would take to feed them into the machines."

"Good point…We could take them to the Belton Redemption Center. They take returnables. It's what, a mile or so from here?"

"Something like that. Good idea. That should work."

"But, another thing," Tommy said. "We're probably not going to have time to collect the cans *and* bring them to the redemption center in the same day. We'll be doing good just to empty all of the barrels on Saturdays. We'll need a place to store the cans before we turn them in. Some type of holding area."

Kirk glanced around the inside of the shed. "I don't think that's going to be a problem."

"You mean here? The shed?"

"Yep."

"Good call." Kirk took another bite of his apple and chewed thoughtfully for a moment. "You really think we can pull this off?"

"I don't know, but I think it's like Mr. Hardwick said: 'Sometimes you just have to go out and give it a try.' I think this is one of those times."

"Saturday is going to be a long day," said Kirk.

"You got that right."

"Well, we sure got a lot accomplished this afternoon."

"Yep. But we've got a long way to go yet."

"That we do, partner."

Chapter 10

All In A Day's Work

Kirk could see his breath in the air when the Hartwell's station wagon pulled into the driveway at 7:30 Saturday morning.

"I can't believe I let you con me into doing this," Jenna complained. "I could be home in bed sleeping right now."

"You'll be glad you drove us when I'm doing your dish duty tonight," Tommy reassured her.

"I'll bring you guys to all of the schools *except* for the high school. I'm not pulling up in front of the high school in this thing."

"But—"

"*No*," Jenna said firmly. "I'll drop you guys off a block before the high school— not an inch closer."

"Okay, okay. We'll take what we can get."

Kirk hopped in the back seat and they were off.

The first stop was Jacob's Hardware Store. Jenna put the back seat down while Tommy and Kirk went inside to pick up the first set of barrels.

"Glad to be rid of `em," Mr. Jacob told them. "See you fellas at closing time. Save some energy for my floors."

"Thanks Mr. Jacob, will do. See you at six."

Bacon Davis Elementary was the first stop after the hardware store. Kirk knew the school well. He had attended Bacon Davis from kindergarten through fifth grade. And he had always been on good terms with the janitor, Mr. Greely. Mr. Greely was a kind-natured man, just like Mr. Putnam. Kirk had helped him out a few times.

When he was in fourth grade, a bunch of kids made a mess out of the leaves that Mr. Greely had laboriously raked into piles in front of the school. Kirk helped him rake them back into piles after school. And there was also the time in fifth grade when he helped him move stage props.

Mr. Greely was outside the front office adjusting a door closer when Kirk and Tommy arrived.

"Hey there Mr. Greely," called Kirk.

The janitor lowered his screwdriver and turned around.

"Well, Kirk Atwill! You've grown an inch or two since I last saw you, son!"

"My parents keep telling me the same thing. This is my friend, Tommy."

"Good to meet you Tommy."

"Same here, sir."

Mr. Greely took notice of the shiny green barrel each of them was carrying. "You boys working for that recycling outfit the superintendent's office phoned us about?"

"Yes sir," said Tommy. "Half Profit Recycling."

"Good to see boys your age working. I worked when I was your age too. You don't see as much of that these days. Well, follow me and we'll get those barrels in place."

It took less than ten minutes to place the barrels—one in the teacher's lounge, one in the cafeteria.

"Thanks, Mr. Greely. We'll be back next Saturday morning to empty them if that's okay."

"I'll be here boys. See you then."

It was that easy. A half hour later, after another trip to the hardware store, they were enroute to Casey Hayes Elementary School.

The main entrance to Casey Hayes Elementary was locked when Kirk and Tommy arrived, but the side door was unlocked. They made their way into the building. A few minutes later they were walking down the main corridor with the barrels when they heard footsteps behind them...

"HEY YOU!"

Kirk and Tommy froze...and turned slowly around.

"School's closed! Scram you kids!" The words came from a short, heavyset man in a dark green janitor uniform.

"We're from Half Profit Recycling," Tommy announced. "We're here to drop off a few recycling barrels."

"Sure kid. Good one. Now get lost before I call the cops."

"It's the truth," Kirk said. He held up a barrel and gestured to the Half Profit Recycling sign.

The janitor worked a toothpick from one side of his mouth to the other. He squinted at the barrels.

"We're here to put one in the teacher's lounge, and one in the lunchroom," Tommy informed the man.

The janitor's face reddened. "Says who?"

"Superintendent Stackner, sir."

"Is that so?" the man snickered. "Well, I haven't heard anything about this."

"The superintendent's secretary called the school to let them know we'd be by this morning," Kirk put in.

"Well, I wouldn't know anything about that. I'm filling in for Harry today. He's the regular janitor. He's out sick today. Nobody told me anything about any confounded recycling barrels!"

An idea came to Tommy. "Well sir, you can call Superintendent Stackner on Monday to check if you like…But I don't think he'd be too happy to learn that your school was the only one to refuse the new barrels. Your call."

"…Okay you two. Let's make it quick. I've got work to do."

"I hope Harry is back next week," said Kirk, on their way out of the building ten minutes later.

"Yeah, he's gotta be nicer than that guy."

It was 11:15AM when Tommy's sister pulled over to the curb, two blocks from the high school.

"Last stop. I'm outta here," she said. "Vamoose you two. This is the end of the line."

"Thanks Jen."

"Yeah, thanks a lot for your help this morning," said Kirk.

"Hasta la vista."

Kirk and Tommy unloaded the remaining barrels and lugged them toward the high school as the station wagon disappeared down the road.

"This place is huge," Tommy observed, as they entered the high school. The place was different than the other schools. The hallways were wider, the lockers taller, and there were a lot more classrooms. There were three gymnasiums, and there was even an indoor pool. It was a different world all together.

It took them twenty minutes just to find the locker rooms, another twenty to locate the cafeteria and the teacher's lounge. By noon, the barrels were in place—but the real work had yet to begin. The real work would start next Saturday when they would empty the barrels and remove all of the cans.

"You hungry?" asked Kirk.

"Starved."

"Pizza?"

"Let's go!"

They treated themselves to pizza and Cokes at Belton Pizza. And as they ate, Tommy and Kirk realized they forgot to swing by Horace Clovis Middle School to empty the barrels. It would have to wait.

"Let's hook up with Mr. Putnam before school Monday," said Kirk. "Make arrangements to collect the cans Monday afternoon."

"Sounds like a plan."

They met Mr. Jacob at six o'clock that night and swept and mopped the floors at the hardware store. And on Sunday morning they were back to business. They met at the shed at nine o'clock and spent the better part of the day constructing makeshift wagons for their bikes out of two old strollers and a roll of chicken wire.

As they labored, they worked out some more of the details of the business, calculating how many trash bags they'd need to buy and what the best day would be to deliver the cans to the Belton Redemption Center. Everything else, they'd learn as they went along.

They finished just before three o'clock, then sat down and admired their handiwork. Assembled before them were two box-like contraptions on wheels—each a combination of a stripped down stroller and chicken wire, bound together with bungee cords. The makeshift wagons were quite a sight.

"Not bad," acknowledged Tommy.

"You think they'll work?" inquired Kirk.

"We'll find out next Saturday."

"That we will."

Chapter 11
Breaking The Rules

Every school has rules and one of the rules at Horace Clovis Middle School was that students were not allowed to enter the building before first bell unless they were meeting with a teacher. But the rule was not regularly enforced. That's why Kirk and Tommy thought nothing of trying to locate Mr. Putnam before school Monday morning, coffee in hand.

"HALT!"

They were half way down the front hall. The two of them froze, then slowly did an about-face to see Principal Philbrick glaring down at them.

"And where are you two off to this morning?" He eyed the coffee suspiciously.

Kirk was at a loss for words. But Tommy spoke up.

"We're going to meet with our teacher."

"Which teacher?"

"...Mr. Hardwick," Kirk said. It was partially true. They would have stopped by Mr. Hardwick's office to say hi after they spoke with Mr. Putnam.

"Mr. Hardwick is out sick today," snapped Principal Philbrick. "So, you two head back outside till the bell. And I'll take the coffee. You won't be needing that."

Tommy handed over the coffee.

They caught up with Mr. Putnam at lunch and made arrangements to meet him after school at 4:45, when the teachers were gone. When they arrived that afternoon, Mr. Putnam had already emptied the recycling barrels into trash bags and placed the bags by the side entrance for them.

"We ought to get a gift for Putnam," said Kirk. "He's been a huge help."

"We should get gifts for all of the janitors," Tommy replied.

Kirk nodded in agreement. "Soon as we can afford to."

The rest of the week ticked by. Each day seemed slower than the one before. Saturday seemed an eternity away. The anticipation was killing them. Would the barrels be full on Saturday? Or empty? Would they be able to transport all of the cans from the schools? These were the thoughts that passed through their minds as they waited for Saturday to arrive.

Chapter 12
Collection Day

The November sky was clear, the temperature brisk, as Tommy skidded to a stop at the end of the Atwill's driveway. It was seven o'clock Saturday morning. Kirk was out back in the shed. He was attaching one of the makeshift wagons to his bike.

"Morning," Tommy yawned.

"Hey, Tommy. You ready?"

"You bet."

"Let's get to it."

"Aye-aye captain."

Tommy hitched up the other wagon to his bike and they pedaled off, wagons in tow.

The game plan was simple. They had worked it out during lunch the day before. The two of them would split up. Each would take an elementary school. Then they'd meet back at the shed to drop off the cans before heading off to work Horace Clovis Middle School and the high school together.

They flipped a coin to see who would take which elementary school. Both were a little reluctant about Casey Hayes Elementary after last week's episode. Kirk won the coin toss and chose Bacon Davis Elementary; Tommy frowned, but fair was fair.

Mr. Greely was out front sweeping the walk when Kirk pulled up in front of Bacon Davis Elementary, his wagon in tow. "Nice rig you have there," the janitor remarked. "That's quite a contraption."

"Thanks Mr. Greely. You're my first stop. Guess I'll find out how well it works soon enough."

"Well, I suppose you want to get at those barrels, eh?"

"Yes sir."

"Follow me."

Mr. Greely opened the door to the teacher's lounge. Kirk walked over to the Half Profit Recycling barrel and removed a bag from his hip pocket. The janitor helped him pry the lid off…Three empty soda cans lay on the bottom. It was a start—but not a very good one.

"The soda vending machine broke last week," Mr. Greely explained. "Maybe you fared better in the cafeteria."

Kirk tossed the three cans into the bag, placed the lid back on the barrel, and followed the janitor to the cafeteria. Being in the school brought back memories. Kirk passed by three of his old classrooms on the way. The place seemed so small compared to the middle school; it was almost as if the walls were closing in on him.

Kirk's face creased in a smile when they pried the lid off the barrel in the cafeteria. It was nearly full. Mr. Greely helped him empty the contents of the barrel into a bag.

"I'd say you're off to a good start," he announced.

"Thanks for your help," Kirk said, tossing the bag over his shoulder. "See you the same time next Saturday?"

"I'll be here. Always happy to help out a Bacon Davis graduate."

"Thanks again, Mr. Greely."

Back outside, Kirk tossed the bag into the wagon and headed home to the shed.

Across town, Tommy was just arriving at Casey Hayes Elementary. Something in his stomach stirred as he neared the school. He vividly remembered the encounter with the substitute janitor the week before. A custodian in a green uniform was changing a light bulb outside the front office when Tommy entered the building. The guy glanced down from his step ladder as Tommy approached. The name tag on his shirt read, Harry. "Can I help you?" the man asked in a pleasant tone.

Tommy breathed a sigh of relief. Even though Tommy didn't know him, it was good to have Harry back.

"Hi sir. I'm from Half Profit Recycling. I'm here to empty the recycling barrels."

"Oh yes. I've been expecting you. They told me someone would be stopping by…but I guess I was expecting someone a little—"

"Older?" Tommy offered.

"Yes."

"I've heard that before."

"I'll bet. The name's Harry," the man said, offering his hand.

Tommy reached up and shook the man's hand. "Tommy Hartwell. Nice to meet you, Harry."

"Likewise young man. Now, let's see. If my memory is correct, one of those barrels is in the teacher's lounge, and there's another in the lunchroom."

"That's right."

"Let me just finish up here for a second. I'll give you a hand."

"Thanks Harry."

Five minutes later they were outside the teacher's lounge. Harry pulled a ring of keys from his belt and fiddled with them. "There it is," he said, grasping a brass-colored key. He inserted the key into the door lock and opened the door. The two of them stepped into the teacher's lounge.

Tommy walked over to the recycling barrel and shook it. Some cans rattled inside. He popped the lid off and emptied ten cans into a bag.

The barrel in the cafeteria was a different story—it was full. With Harry's help, Tommy emptied the contents of the barrel into the bag.

"Well, that's all for this week," said Tommy. "Thanks for your help, Harry!"

"Pleasure was mine. Good luck now."

"Okay if I come back same time next week?" Tommy asked.

"You bet. I'll be here."

"Okay, see you then Harry."

Kirk was in front of the shed when Tommy pulled up. Tommy had had a good morning too, Kirk observed. His load was big, maybe even larger than Kirk's.

"Looking good," Kirk said.

"Looks like you did pretty well yourself," Tommy replied, glancing at the pile of cans on the floor of the shed.

"All in a morning's work."

They removed the bag from Tommy's cart and brought it inside. Then they spilled the contents onto the pile that Kirk had started.

"Not a bad start," Tommy acknowledged.

"How many you figure we have?" Kirk wondered.

"I really have no idea."

"Well, we should probably get back at it."

"Yep. Let's go see Mr. Putnam."

Kirk glanced at his watch. They were making good time. It was just past ten as they headed off the middle school. Horace Clovis Middle School wasn't a far ride. Mr. Putnam had already emptied the barrels and left the bags out for them. They made it back to the shed in a half hour. The pile on the shed floor grew significantly when they emptied the Horace Clovis Middle School load—the contents of two and a half barrels. The two cafeteria barrels had been full; the one in the teacher's lounge had been half full.

"Not bad," said Kirk. "I wonder how many we have now."

"No idea," replied Tommy.

"And still more to come," said Kirk. "We should probably head over to the high school now."

"Let's move out." It took them ten minutes to reach the high school. They went to the teacher's lounge first. The door was unlocked. Kirk and Tommy went inside and made their way over to the recycling barrel. They pried the lid off…and saw the barrel was full of soda cans.

Tommy whistled. "I guess high school teachers drink more soda."

"Maybe," said Kirk. "But maybe it's that there are more teachers here." Given the size of the place, there had to be. Every kid in town funneled into the high school eventually. It was by far the largest school in the district. And the community college had a night school program there. Night school teachers probably used the teacher's lounge too.

They emptied the barrel, then made their way to the cafeteria. Cans were poking through the slots in the recycling barrel lids. And beside the barrels were two trash bags full of cans. It seemed they had been helped out by a janitor once again.

Tommy whistled. "Would you look at that!"

"I think we're going to make some money here," Kirk said excitedly.

"And we're going to need more barrels," Tommy observed.

They emptied the barrels into bags and took all of the bags outside and tossed them in a pile by their bikes. Then they made their way back inside to the hallway outside the boys locker room. The barrel beside the soda machine was full. The one by the girls' locker room was the same. They combined the contents of both barrels into bags, made their way back outside, and loaded the bags onto the wagon.

It was their biggest haul yet, but they were prepared. They tied each load down with heavy duty string.

The two of them were surely quite a sight as they pedaled away, the trash bags piled up high in the wagons behind them. To get to Kirk's house, they had to cut through downtown, across Main Street. Motorists slowed down to look at them. A man mowing his lawn stopped and looked at them. A group of kids playing basketball stopped their game. Kirk and Tommy didn't mind the attention. It felt good.

It was past noon when they reached the shed. They emptied the bags onto the pile inside the shed, then stepped back and looked at it. The pile was taller than them. There were some nonreturnable cans and bottles mixed in, along with milk cartons and yogurt containers, but they could be sorted out easy enough.

"What do you figure they're worth?" Kirk pondered.

"I don't know, but I'm looking forward to finding out."

"Same here," said Kirk. "You hungry?"

"Starved."

"Pizza?"

"Let's go."

*****

Kirk stumbled into the dining room when he got back from the hardware store that evening. His mother was just putting dinner on the table. Kirk took a seat at the table beside his father.

"Long day, eh, son?"

"Uh huh. Looks like tomorrow's going to be a long one too."

"You're working tomorrow?" asked Mrs. Atwill. "On Sunday?"

"Yep." Kirk yawned. "Today we collected. Tomorrow we sort and pack the cans."

"Sounds like you've got it all figured out," his father commented.

"We're just kind of figuring it out as we go along."

"Looks like you're not the only working man in the house anymore," Mrs. Atwill kidded her husband.

"So I see."

Kirk's mother placed a plate of spaghetti and meatballs before him. Kirk dug in.

"Whoa!" said his mother. "Easy does it. Slow down. You don't want to get indigestion."

"Sorry," Kirk said. His eyelids were getting heavy now.

"Physical work will do that to you," his father remarked.

After he finished his meal, Kirk asked, "Can I be excused?"

"And miss dessert?" his mother replied. "It's your favorite—apple pie and vanilla ice cream."

"I'm tired. Can you save my portion for tomorrow?"

"My, you *are* tired. Sure honey. We'll save you a piece."

"Goodnight Mom. Night Dad."

Kirk was fast asleep five minutes later.

Chapter 13
The Recycling Business

Sunday morning. The sky was overcast; rain pelted the side of the house. A good day to sleep in. Kirk was still asleep when his father tapped on his bedroom door. He groaned and slowly rolled over. The clock radio on his bureau read eight o'clock.

"Tommy Hartwell is downstairs to see you."

Kirk squinted and rubbed the sleep from his eyes. He could have slept for hours more. His body was stiff; his hands ached. His arms and legs ached. He slowly dragged himself out of bed, pulled on a pair of jeans and a sweatshirt, then stumbled downstairs.

Tommy was at the kitchen table eating a corn muffin. "I thought you were gonna sleep the day away," he said, as Kirk padded into the kitchen.

"I could have...What time did you get up?" Kirk yawned and rubbed his eyes.

"Been up since six-thirty. I'm an early riser."

Kirk joined Tommy at the table. His mother placed a mug of hot chocolate before each of them. "Thanks for the breakfast, Mrs. Atwill," Tommy said. "That corn muffin was the best I've ever had."

"You're quite welcome, Tommy. Glad you enjoyed it. It's *always* nice to hear a compliment," she said, giving Kirk a friendly nod.

The mountain of beverage containers inside the shed seemed to loom even higher than the day before. "Where should we start?" Kirk wondered out loud.

"Good question."

They decided it would be best to separate beverage containers into two categories: ten-cent returnables and non-returnables.

They placed two barrels beside the pile and placed a bag in each one. Then they began the laborious process of sorting through the pile. When each barrel was full, they pulled the bag out, tied it, and tossed it outside. Then they started the process all over again.

They finished up just before noon. The pile was gone; not a single bottle or can could be found on the floor.

"Not much more we can do today," Kirk acknowledged. "The redemption center is closed Sundays."

"Yep, we'll head there tomorrow after school."

"It's probably going to take more than one afternoon to deliver all the cans," Kirk said. "Probably take a few days."

Tommy nodded and glanced up at the sky. It had stopped raining. "You're right," he agreed. "But let's worry about that tomorrow. You up for a game of street hockey? Some of the guys are getting a game going down at the tennis courts this afternoon.

The recreation department just took the nets down for the season."

"You bet. Enough work for one weekend. You know what they say about all work and no play…"

Anyone watching Kirk and Tommy play street hockey that afternoon would have likely guessed they were just like the other players. Just two eighth-graders who spent their free time playing street hockey and doing whatever else it was kids their age did in their free time. They never would have guessed that the two of them were budding entrepreneurs who owned a business.

*****

Tommy and Kirk met at the shed Monday after school. They loaded bags of ten-cent deposit cans onto the makeshift wagons and strapped them down. Then they began the slow trek to the Belton Redemption Center. Once again, people stopped what they were doing and stared as the two of them pedaled by with the strange wagons in tow.

The redemption center was housed in an old brick building in the mill district. The building had formerly been a textile mill. An older woman was seated at the front desk when they walked in.

She looked up from her paperwork and arched her eyebrows when she saw the two boys in front of her. Each boy was holding two bags of containers.

"What do we have here, boys?"

"Cans ma'am."

"Are they all returnables—10¢ deposit cans?"

"That's right."

"Right through there," she said, pointing to a wide doorway across the room.

"Thanks ma'am."

The doorway led to a much larger room. A heavyset man was sitting at a desk reading a magazine when Kirk and Tommy walked in. The name tag over his front shirt pocket read: Otis. Monday afternoons were apparently slow.

Otis didn't look up, just kept on reading. After a few seconds, Tommy fake-coughed. The guy finally put the magazine down.

"What have you got there, boys?"

"Cans, sir."

Otis sighed and slowly stood, pulling his belt up. "Follow me." They followed the man across the room, passing by large bins of beverage containers. Otis led them to a long counter on the far side of the room. Then he walked behind the counter and faced them.

"Together or separate?" he asked.

Kirk and Tommy glanced at each other. "Huh?"

"You want them altogether on one slip—or on separate slips?"

"Oh, together."

"Okay, spill 'em," the man said, motioning to the counter. Tommy opened up a bag and spilled the contents onto the counter.

Kirk did the same. Tommy was about to empty a third bag on the counter when Otis shouted, "Stop! Let me get caught up with these ones first."

Otis slowly picked through the pile, inspecting each can before tossing it into a large bin behind the counter. When the pile was gone, he instructed them to unload the other bags onto the counter. Then he repeated the process. When he finished, he handed Kirk a slip.

"Give that to Doris at the front desk. She'll get you your money."

"Thanks sir."

"No need to call me sir."

"Yes sir, er—Otis."

Doris glanced at the slip when Kirk handed it to her. "Is that it boys, or are you bringing more today?" she asked.

"More on the way," Tommy informed her.

"Well then, keep the slip for now," she said, handing it back. "Just give me all of your slips together when you're done, and we'll get you squared away all at once. Easier that way."

"Will do."

When Tommy and Kirk returned an hour later with another load, Doris was gone. They took the bags into the back room. Otis was sitting down at his desk. He was engrossed in a magazine. He raised his eyebrows. "Back again, eh?"

"Actually, this isn't the last of them. You'll be seeing

more of us this week," Tommy said.

"Is that right?"

Kirk and Tommy spilled the contents of the bags onto the counter. Otis went to work. Afterward, he gave them another slip, and said, "Doris is gone for the rest of the day. She's the only one that works the register. She'll be back on Friday. Just hang onto your slips, give them to her then."

They returned to the redemption center the following afternoon with the rest of cans. And they went back once more on Friday afternoon to give Doris the slips.

"Oh my," she said. "You boys have been busy. She stood up and made her way to the cash register. Doris punched a few buttons on the cash register. The drawer popped open. She extracted some bills and coins and handed them to Kirk. Kirk counted the money and smiled.

"Thanks ma'am!"

"Don't spend it all in one place," Doris advised.

Outside, Kirk yelled. "Oh yeah!"

"How sweet it is!"

"Remember though," Kirk said. "Half goes to charity."

Tommy's eyebrows arched. "Oh yeah, that's right."

"I was thinking we could donate half of this week's profits to the thrift shop downtown. They're nonprofit—all the money they earn goes to helping people in need. My mother volunteers there. Maybe we could stop by the arcade for a few games after."

"Let's go!"

A hanging bell on the back of the thrift shop's entry door announced their arrival. An older woman stood behind the counter. "You boys looking for anything in particular? We just got some hockey equipment in. It's at the back of the store."

"Actually, we're here to make a donation." The words came from Kirk.

The woman smiled. It made her day when kids came in to donate change. "The donation jar is right over there," she said, pointing to a quart jar the end of the counter.

She watched as Kirk and Tommy made their way over to the jar...and her eyes grew wide when Kirk removed the roll of bills from his pocket. He peeled off half the bills and stuffed them into the jar along with some change.

"My goodness, that's mighty kind of you," the woman exclaimed. Most kids just dropped a dime or maybe a quarter in the jar.

"Our pleasure, ma'am. You'll see us again."

*****

The next few weeks were basically a repeat. They emptied the barrels at each school on Saturday, sorted and packed them on Sunday, then brought the cans to the redemption center the following week and deposited half of their earnings into the thrift shop's donation jar.

During their third week in business, they set up an office in the shed. It wasn't much, just an old desk and two folding chairs, all of which had been salvaged from the curb on trash day. On top of the desk rested a calculator and a used table lamp. The lamp was powered by an extension cord they ran from an outside outlet on the back of Kirk's house. They kept their earnings in a metal cash box beneath a floorboard in the shed.

During their fourth week in business, they purchased a can masher. This allowed them to get more cans in each bag and reduce the number of trips to the redemption center. They also bought a used wash tub for cleaning cans. Otis was finicky about cans that had "too much crud on `em."

By this point, they had worked out a type of honor system with Otis, where they'd simply tell him how many cans were in each bag. It gave the man more reading time.

The Saturday collections were becoming more routine now, and by the end of December, things were quite manageable. Everything was going smoothly. They had learned some of the ins and outs of the business in a relatively short period of time. All in all, things were looking good...but that was before Lyle Cutler entered the scene.

Chapter 14
Double Detention

School Secretary, June Tidwell, couldn't believe her eyes. It was the first day back from Christmas break, and a pizza delivery man had just passed by the front office. He was headed toward the cafeteria. This was a first. In all her fifteen years as school secretary, nobody ever had a pizza delivered to the cafeteria.

Heads turned in the cafeteria when the pizza delivery man entered.

"Over here!" Tommy called, waving the guy over.

The pizza delivery man waded through the tables and chairs. All eyes were on him as he approached Tommy and Kirk's table.

He uncased the pizza—a large triple cheese with pepperoni and onions. Then he set it down on the table.

"Thanks, my good man," said Tommy, handing the guy a wad of bills. Keep the change."

The guy counted the money and stuffed it in his shirt pocket. "*Thank you*."

There were five kids at the table, including Tommy and Kirk, but as Tommy started doling out slices, the other seats quickly filled. Tommy had to cut each piece in half in order to have enough to go around. Their lunch table crowd grew that day.

They ordered two pizzas the following day. Kirk paid this time. Kids crammed around the table in anticipation. Kirk and Tommy enjoyed the attention. It was as if they had become instant celebrities. The lunchroom crowd was louder than usual with all of the excitement. The roar of the crowd could be heard all the way down the hall in the front office. And Principal Philbrick heard it from his office.

"What's all the commotion about, June?

"Ummm…I'm not sure sir…Sounds like it's coming from the cafeteria."

"Hmmm."

Kirk was handing out the last slice when the lunchroom crowd suddenly grew quiet.

"Ahem!"

Kirk slowly turned around. The principal was glaring down at him.

"Who ordered the pizza!?" he inquired.

Tommy and Kirk exchanged glances.

"Uh…We did sir."

"You two again, eh? I had a feeling you two were up to something. Well, tell you what. You've just earned yourselves *double detention*! This is strictly against school rules."

"*Double* detention?" questioned Tommy.

"That's right," Philbrick said. "Lunch detention *and* after school detention—for a week."

Lunch detention wasn't so bad. That just meant they had to eat lunch in a classroom rather than the cafeteria. You could still buy lunch in the cafeteria; you just couldn't eat it there with everyone else. But *after school detention* was another story.

"Report to my office at the close of school today, gentlemen."

"Yes sir," stammered Tommy.

"I guess the pizza wasn't such a good idea," Kirk said, after the principal left.

"Yeah, I guess we kind of over did it," Tommy admitted. What they didn't know was that things were about to get worse.

*****

Lyle Cutler exceeded in the art of bullying. The eighth-grader was notorious for hassling kids, taking lunch money, and just being a general nuisance. And he took notice of Kirk emptying the pizza boxes into the trash can during eighth grade lunch period.

Kirk was at his locker getting a book after fifth period. The locker door was open; it obstructed his view down the hall. When he shut the locker door he saw Lyle Cutler. The kid was casually leaning against the locker next to Kirk's. Lyle was clad in dark jeans, combat boots, and a sleeveless skull & cross bones t-shirt.

"I need a loan," Lyle said.

"H-huh?"

"I need you to loan me ten bucks."

Kirk nervously looked up at the bully. Somehow, he doubted the kid was looking for a "loan." More than likely, he'd never see a dime if he handed money over to this clown.

"...Sorry, I'm tapped out," Kirk lied.

"I don't need it *today*," the bully replied. "I need it *tomorrow*. I'll be here same time tomorrow afternoon to collect it. Just after fifth period."

Kirk stood frozen in place as Lyle turned and strutted down the hall, off to torment some other student no doubt. The thought of meeting up with the kid the following day was not pleasant. Kirk guessed that if he gave Lyle ten dollars, it wouldn't be the end of it. The kid would surely be back for more. That's what had happened to his cousin at his school in Ohio. This bully took his lunch money every day for three months.

Tommy walked over to Kirk's locker. "What was Lyle Cutler talking to you about?" he asked.

"You know him?"

"I know *of* him. He's bad news."

"Yeah, no kidding. He wants me to lend him ten dollars."

"Don't do it."

"I might not have a choice—in case you didn't notice, he's about a foot taller than me. Probably fifty pounds heavier than me too."

"Don't worry about it," said Tommy. "Just avoid him. He'll probably move on and try to intimidate someone else tomorrow.

Easy for you to say. He's not after you.

*****

"What did you two do?" Mrs. Tidwell whispered. School had just let out and Kirk and Tommy were sitting on the bench outside Principal Philbrick's office.

"Um…We had pizza delivered to the cafeteria," Tommy told her.

The woman raised her hand to her mouth. "Oh my. That was you two?"

Kirk nodded. "Yes ma'am. Unfortunately."

Just then, Principal Philbrick opened his office door. "Step inside boys."

Kirk and Tommy had never before set foot in the principal's office. But they had heard the rumors about the place. Word was that Philbrick had a hoard of confiscated items in his office—everything from Silly Putty to skateboards. Kirk guessed the stuff must be in the closet. All they saw was a coat rack, a book case, a large oak desk at the back of the room, and two small wooden chairs before it.

"Take a seat, gentlemen."

Kirk and Tommy sat down and faced the principal. The man reached into a drawer and removed a pad—a pad of detention slips. He ripped off two sheets and scribbled on them. "If I had my way, you'd start your detention today," he barked. "But school rules mandate that your parents sign these before you serve detention." He handed each of them a detention notice.

"Have your parents sign these when you get home today. I'll expect them on my desk tomorrow morning first thing. Just *after* first bell. Your after school detention will start tomorrow. You'll be helping Mr. Putnam each afternoon this week. I'll see to it that he puts you two to work."

Kirk and Tommy did their best not to smile. Detention wasn't going to be so bad. They'd be glad to help Mr. Putnam. If there was one person they wouldn't mind helping it was Mr. Putnam.

"You find this amusing do you boys?"

"Uh...no sir," replied Tommy.

"Very well then. That will be all.

"Yes sir."

*****

"Not hungry?" Tommy inquired, during lunch detention the following day. He had walked across the hall and joined Kirk in his homeroom.

"No."

Tommy seemed to read his partner's thoughts. "Worried about Lyle?"

"Yeah. Wouldn't you be?"

"Like I said, just avoid him."

"Believe me, I plan to...but I can't get away with that forever. The school's not that big a place. Plus, the kid's going to be at my locker after fifth period."

"Listen," said Tommy. "This guy's big—but he's not

bigger than *both* of us together. We'll just stick together. He won't bother you if we're both there."

For the first time that day, Kirk smiled. And it was then that he realized just how glad he was to have Tommy Hartwell for a partner.

"Thanks Tommy."

Tommy shrugged. "What are partners for?"

Kirk ate some lunch. He was feeling a little better, though Lyle Cutler was still at the forefront of his thoughts. Tommy and Kirk didn't have the same classes. Running into Lyle Cutler solo was not a pleasant thought at all.

Kirk's heart raced at the end of fifth period. The time had come. He slowly made his way down the hall to his locker… Tommy was leaning against it.

"No sign of him yet," Tommy declared.

"Maybe he skipped school today," Kirk guessed, glancing around.

"Maybe."

A few minutes passed. There was still no sign of Lyle. Then the sixth period bell sounded. *Maybe I worried for nothing,* Kirk thought, on his way to social studies. The heavy feeling he had felt in his stomach eased up. And when there was still no sign of Lyle after sixth period, Kirk started feeling altogether better.

But then, after the dismissal bell, Kirk was at his locker putting his books away. When he closed the door… Lyle was there, just like the day before.

"Avoiding me today, eh Atwill?" Lyle sneered. He held out his right hand, palm up. "Ten bucks. I need it now."

"Uh...I... don't... have any money."

Lyle's face reddened. "Yeah right! You had money for two large pizzas yesterday. And I've seen that mountain bike you ride. You've got money all right—enough to loan me ten bucks. Now fork it over!"

"...R-really...I...don't...have...any— "

"Sure you do," said Lyle, cutting him off. The kid stepped forward, backed Kirk up against his locker.

"I'm going to ask you just once more," said Lyle, jabbing a finger into Kirk's chest. "And if you don't have the answer I'm looking for, we're going to take a little walk to the restroom, where we can discuss this further. Then, I'm taking your bike for a little ride."

Kirk froze. His lower lip quivered. A group of kids had gathered around them. Kirk searched frantically for Tommy but he was no where to be seen.

"So, what's it gonna be!?" Lyle punched the locker just to the right of Kirk's head; Kirk winced. The sound echoed down the hall, attracting spectators.

A small group of students gathered around them. "Last chance," sneered, Lyle, pointing to the boys' restroom across the hall. He didn't see Tommy approaching from behind. Tommy was silent as a fox. Kirk had never been so glad to see his partner.

Tommy snuck up behind Lyle. He removed his jacket and dropped down to the floor. He got on his hands and knees. Then he laid his jacket out on the floor behind him.

"Last chance!" barked Lyle. Tommy looked up at Kirk and nodded. Then he shouted: "NOW!"

Kirk braced his back against the locker and pushed Lyle Cutler with all of his might. Lyle tumbled backwards over Tommy…and landed on the floor. The crowd cheered. Everything had happened so fast.

"Oldest trick in the book." said Tommy. This brought more laughs from the crowd.

Lyle was too surprised to respond at first. He wasn't hurt—there was a thick rubber mat on the floor in the locker area, and Tommy's jacket had cushioned the impact as well.

Lyle's face turned beet red as he heard the laughter. But before he could make a move, Tommy and Kirk pounced on him. They pinned him to the floor. Lyle was helpless.

"You mess with Kirk, you mess with me too," Tommy whispered in Lyle's ear. "Got it?"

Lyle nodded, fear in his eyes now.

Just then, footsteps could be heard approaching from the down the hall.

"Philbrick's coming," someone warned. The crowd disbursed. Kirk and Tommy got up and mixed in with the crowd. Lyle stood up slowly, looked around as if in a fog.

"Fighting again, Mr. Cutler? Let's discuss this in my office, young man."

Lyle Cutler was no longer a problem.

That afternoon, Kirk and Tommy helped Mr. Putnam empty wastebaskets in the classrooms. After that, they swept the hallway floors with push-brooms, stocked toilet paper in the restrooms, and washed restroom mirrors. They did this each day of their detention that week.

After the detention was behind them, things returned to normal. The Lyle problem had been resolved. And everything was going smoothly...They had no way of knowing that things wouldn't remain that way long.

Chapter 15
Help Wanted

Mayor Whitten pulled into the parking lot at Casey Hayes Elementary School at 7:30AM on the third Monday in January. His daughter was a third-grader at the school. He was there for a parent-teacher conference. The mayor pulled up the collar on his overcoat against the cold January wind as he made his way across the school's parking lot.

The mayor was ten minutes early. His daughter's teacher's door was closed when he arrived. With ten minutes to spare, he strolled down the corridor, observing the art-work that adorned the walls. About halfway down the hall, he saw the teacher's lounge door was open. He peeked in…and a shiny green recycling barrel caught his attention. This was good to see. The topic of recycling had just come up at a staff meeting. Belton was behind some neighboring towns when it came to recycling. The mayor took a small notepad from his suit coat pocket and jotted down the phone number on the sign on the barrel. The phone number for Half Profit Recycling.

*****

"We got a call from the mayor," Tommy told Kirk the following morning before school.

Kirk rolled his eyes. Tommy could be a joker sometimes.

"I'm not kidding," Tommy said. "He left a message. Here, listen for yourself. I taped it." Tommy pulled his tape recorder from his jacket pocket and pushed the play button. Kirk's eyebrows lifted when he heard the mayor's message.

"I guess we need to return his call."

"Right after school."

"Could you make the call again?" Kirk asked.

"Actually, I have someone else in mind."

"Who?"

"My grandmother."

"Huh?"

"Trust me."

"Okay."

*****

Tommy updated Kirk on the way to his grandmother's house after school. Told him how his grandmother was friends with the woman who worked at Helping Hands, and that the woman mentioned two boys who came to the thrift store each week to donate money. One of them fit Tommy's description. When his grandmother confronted him, Tommy told her about the business. She said to let her know if she could ever be of help.

They walked along the sidewalk that paralleled Main Street for three blocks, and then turned right onto Partridge Road.

Halfway down the road, Tommy stopped in front of a purple bungalow with green trim and headed up the front walk. Kirk had passed by the house before on his trash route, always figured an artist lived there. The door was painted with vibrant flowers—as was the 1969 Volkswagen Beetle in the driveway.

Tommy knocked on the door and a few moments later a woman came to the door and opened it. She was clad in flare jeans and a colorful tie dye shirt and a leather fringed vest. Her long grayish-black hair was held back by a beaded headband.

"Thomas!"

"Hi Grandma. This is my friend, Kirk."

"Hello Kirk. Come on in guys."

The aroma of incense permeated their senses as they entered the house. They followed Tommy's grandmother through a beaded curtain just beyond the foyer and entered the living room.

"Have a seat," she said, gesturing to a couch.

Tommy's grandmother sat down in a colossal bean bag chair across from them. As Tommy and his grandmother chatted, Kirk took in the tie dye flower mural that filled the far wall. Then, Tommy got down to business. "Grandma, we'll take you up on that offer to help us."

The woman smiled. "Far out. What can I do?"

"Well…we need to call the mayor. And we were hoping you might be able to call him on our behalf."

"That's it? Hand me the phone."

"Ahem…Yes, Mayor Whitten please…Hello sir. This is Half Profit Recycling… Yes… Yes…How many town facilities are there? Yes sir, we can handle that… Sure, we can have barrels placed in each location by then. No problem… Thank you sir… Just give us a call if we can be of any further help, and thanks for choosing Half Profit Recycling."

Kirk and Tommy looked her anxiously. "Talk to us, Grandma."

"Well, you're going to need a lot more barrels—the town has sixteen other buildings in addition to the schools. The mayor wants a barrel in each one!"

"Yaaah!"

"You two are to meet the town's facilities manager two weeks from Friday at 12:30 at Rosie's Coffee Shop. He's going to get you into each building."

"That day will work well. It's an early release day," Tommy commented. "Thanks Grandma!"

"Yeah, thanks Mrs. Hartwell," said Kirk.

"Glad to help out. Let me know how it goes."

"Will do."

Kirk furrowed his brow on the walk home. "This is beyond our ability you know," he said. "We're stretched out as it is."

"I know, but think of the potential if we can make it work."

"We're going to need some help on this one."

"Yes," Tommy agreed. "We need to find someone that can drive…preferably someone with a truck."

"Know any candidates?"

"Nope…but we could place a help wanted ad in the *The Belton Times*."

"Good idea. Let's head over there after school and place an ad."

The ad ran in the Friday edition of *The Belton Times*:

Recycling Worker Needed

Must have driver's license and own truck.

(555) 555-5699

The advertisement generated three calls the following week. Kirk and Tommy scheduled interviews for Friday afternoon after school—a week before they were to meet with the town's facilities manager. The first candidate was a heavyset guy in his forties. He parked his dump truck along the curb in front of the Atwill's house. Then he walked up the front steps and rang the doorbell. "I'm here for an interview," he told Mrs. Atwill.

"Oh. They're being held out back," she said, gesturing to the backyard. "In the shed."

The man's eyebrows shot up. "Thanks ma'am."

The guy made his way across the driveway to the backyard. Then he approached the shed hesitantly. Kirk and Tommy were inside. They had just pulled two sodas from the cooler, when they heard the knock on the door.

"Come in," said Tommy. "The door's open."

The man entered cautiously. He looked around the shed and glanced at Kirk and Tommy. "Is your father around?" he asked. "I'm here for an interview with Half-Profit Recycling."

Kirk and Tommy exchanged glances. "That's us," Kirk told the man. "The interview is with us. We're the owners."

"That's right," Tommy assured the man.

The guy looked baffled. He took his cap off and scratched his head. Then he smiled and began to laugh. "That's a good one," he said. "Good to see you boys have a sense of humor. But really, where's your father? Or is it your uncle perhaps?"

"It's like we said," Tommy confirmed. "We're the owners. The interview is with us."

"*You two* are the owners? Haw! I've heard some good ones in my day, but this takes the cake. You're not putting me on?"

"No sir."

"Wait till the boys down at the club hear about this!" The man walked out, went back to his truck and drove away.

The second candidate pulled up in a shiny new pickup truck twenty minutes later. He was a tall, wiry man. The fellow was well-groomed; he wore a white-collared shirt with a tie and slacks. Like the first candidate, he knocked on the Atwill's front door and was directed out back to the shed.

At first, Tommy and Kirk thought the guy might be mute. The man didn't utter a word when he stepped into the shed, just stared at them, bewildered. Then he said, "I believe I've made a mistake." And that was it. The guy just turned around and left.

Twenty-five minutes later, the third and final candidate, a nineteen-year-old college student, pulled up in an old pickup truck. The body was pocked with rust; springs poked up through the torn vinyl seat cover. He wore a t-shirt and jeans, torn at the knees. And he found the shed on his own. He was the only one of the three candidates to note the Half Profit Recycling Headquarters sign over the shed's door.

He knocked on the door.

"Come on in."

The kid walked in and stood before Kirk and Tommy.

"I'm Jeremy. Jeremy Mathews. I'm here to interview for the job."

Kirk and Tommy stood up. "I'm Kirk. And this is Tommy. Good to meet you, Jeremy." They shook hands with the job applicant.

"Same here. So, you two work for Half Profit Recycling?"

"…We're the owners," said Tommy.

"No kidding? Cool." Jeremy didn't flinch, didn't even seem surprised.

"Care for a soda?" Kirk offered.

"Sure."

Tommy and Kirk exchanged glances and gave each other a nod. They had found their man.

*****

The plan was for Jeremy to pick up Kirk and Tommy at school at 12:15 that Friday afternoon. From there, they'd head over to Rosie's Coffee Shop and meet up with the town's facilities manager. Jeremy was right on time. They made it to Rosie's by 12:30. But there was no sign of the facilities manager. The man was apparently running late.

They sat down in a booth along the far wall. The waitress stopped by the booth a few minutes later, pot of coffee in hand. "Coffee?" she asked Jeremy.

"No thanks. I don't do caffeine. I'll take a hot chocolate though."

"Make that three hot chocolates," said Tommy.

"Coming right up." Before she left, the waitress looked over at over at Kirk and Tommy. "Aren't you two supposed to be in school?" she smiled.

"Early release day," Kirk explained.

Ten minutes later, a tall, rail-thin man stepped into the diner; he wore tan pants and a matching shirt with a town emblem and a name tag that read: WALT.

"Must be the guy," Tommy guessed.

Most of the lunch crowd had already left. The man worked his way over to their table. "You with the recycling outfit?" he asked Jeremy.

"That's us," Jeremy replied.

"I'm Walter Biggse, the town's facilities manager. I see you've got some helpers."

"Actually, it's the other way around—I'm their helper."

The man wrinkled his forehead. "Huh?"

"I work for them," Jeremy said, gesturing to Kirk and Tommy. "They're the owners."

"Uh…huh…"

The waitress came over just then. "Hey Walt. The usual?"

"No time today. I'm running late. A pipe burst over at the recreation building. Set me back a bit."

"Well, perhaps we'll see you for breakfast tomorrow. Blueberry pancake special. Bye all."

After the waitress left, Walt said, "Well, I guess it would be best if you follow me."

"Will do Walt."

The first stop was Belton Public Library. There was a small single-room café on the first floor that sold coffee, donuts and sandwiches. It also had a soda machine. Kirk, Tommy, and Jeremy got out of the truck and went inside. Jeremy carried a barrel. They placed it beside the soda machine in the café. Walter Biggse waited outside in his green town sedan, talking on his two-way radio.

After that came the police station. Biggse went inside with them this time. When the four of them walked in, a lieutenant at the front desk eyed Tommy and Kirk. Tommy seemed to read the guy's mind.

"Early release day, sir. We're here to place a recycling barrel."

Biggse nodded to the officer. "That's right, lieutenant. Dropping off recycling barrels at all the town buildings today. Where would you like it?"

The officer pointed down the hallway. "Just around the corner. There's a room off the kitchen. That's where we eat. Probably as good a place as any."

Five minutes later they were back in the truck. The next stop was the Belton Fire Station. There, they placed a barrel in the room off the kitchen. After that came Belton Public Works, the town hall, the ice arena, and a number of smaller town sites. By four o'clock they had placed all the barrels.

"Quittin' time," announced Biggse.

They thanked the facilities manager. And Jeremy dropped off Kirk first, and then Tommy. Tommy got home just before five o'clock. He was sitting at his desk in his room when the phone rang—the business phone. Tommy picked up the receiver.

"Half Profit Recycling, Thomas speaking... Yes sir... Hello, Mr. Steibner... Yes...Sure, we can be there tomorrow morning...Eight o'clock is fine....How many?...Uh... yeah, that's not a problem...Okay, we'll be there at eight tomorrow morning...Thank you sir."

Tommy's jaw dropped as he hung up; there was a stunned look on his face. He called Kirk. Kirk picked up on the first ring. "Hello?"

"You're not going to believe who just called."

"You got me."

"Mr. Steibner. Of Steibner Properties?"

"No kidding?"

"I kid you not."

"They own a lot of properties. How do you think they found out about us?"

"Well, Mr. Steibner saw the barrel we dropped off at the ice arena. He just dropped his son off for hockey practice. Turns out he wants our barrels at his properties. Wants us to place them outside each property, next to the dumpsters. We're meeting his property manager tomorrow morning at eight."

"Um, how many buildings *does* Mr. Steibner own?" Kirk inquired.

"Twenty-five," from what he said.

"Twenty-five!?"

"Twenty-five," Tommy confirmed.

"I think our business just doubled. We're going to need to pay another visit to the hardware store. Maybe we can negotiate a line of credit this time."

"Good call."

"Wait. Tomorrow's Saturday," Kirk pointed out. "We've got to empty the barrels at the schools."

"Maybe Jeremy could empty them on Monday."

"Let's see if Jeremy can go with us tomorrow morning."

"Absolutely. I'll give him a call."

"Great!"

When Kirk, Tommy and Jeremy met the property manager from Steibmer Properties the following morning, they learned just how big the Steibner empire was. Steibner Properties owned twelve hundred apartments. Their buildings ranged from small multi-unit brick dwellings to multi-level apartment complexes of more than a hundred units.

Things were pretty crazy over the next few weeks. They hired two neighborhood kids to help sort cans and bottles. And Tommy, Kirk and Jeremy worked well together. Things quickly fell into place. Kirk negotiated a line of credit at Jacob's Hardware Store, and they purchased fifty additional barrels. Tommy printed up signs for the barrels, had them laminated at a print shop so they'd be waterproof. And Jeremy did his share too. Jeremy and his truck were key now. The snow-covered roads were too slippery for bikes at this time of year.

Half Profit Recycling was becoming profitable—very profitable. And the weekly donations to the thrift shop were grow-ing. Yes sir, Half Profit Recycling was steaming right along. And most folks in town, including the mayor, the superintendent of schools and the principal of their school, had no idea that the Business was run by two enterprising eighth-graders. But that was all about to change.

Chapter 16

Playing With The Big Boys

Bartoniy Rubbish Disposal Inc. was the town's largest rubbish disposal company. In fact, aside from a few small haulers, they were the town's *only* rubbish disposal company. Their dark brown dumpsters could be found throughout town. The firm had dumpsters at each of the Steibner properties. And there was a Bartoniy Rubbish Disposal Inc. dumpster at each of the town buildings, including the schools.

The firm had recently diversified. Bartoniy Rubbish Disposal Inc now provided recycling services too. Beside each of their dumpsters were ninety-six gallon recycling toters: one for paper and one for commingled materials such as cans, bottles and other metal, plastic, and glass containers.

Sam Bartoniy, the owner, was quite pleased with his decision to enter the recycling market. It had already significantly increased his profits. But lately, he'd been noticing a reduction in revenue from his commingled recycling containers—the one's for cans and bottles. Like his father before him, Sam Bartoniy kept a sharp eye on his bottom line. Something was up. And he was going to find out what was going on!

The third Thursday in March, Sam Bartoniy climbed into

the passenger seat of Truck #3, and tagged along on the route. He liked to tag along with the drivers now and then. Sometimes it was the only way to get to the bottom of a problem—like this one.

The first stop was Park Ridge Apartments, a Steibner property off Main Street. As the truck backed up to the dumpster, Sam Bartoniy immediately took notice of a new green barrel. It was right beside the dumpster, in close proximity to his recycling toters. "What the —"

Sam Bartoniy hopped out and made his way over to the barrel, more than curious now. The man studied the wording on the front of the new barrel. He knew the competition well, but had never come across Half Profit Recycling before. They were new.

He removed the lid on the Half Profit Recycling barrel... It was chock full of 10¢ deposit bottles and cans. Then he lifted the lid on his commingled recycling toter. It was nearly empty. There were just a few soup cans and plastic milk containers. Sam Bartoniy's face reddened—and he grew even more irate when he discovered more Half Profit Recycling barrels along the route that morning. He was *not* happy. This new recycling company had barrels at all of his sites—including all the town and school buildings. This was costing him! It was time to take action.

When Tommy got home from school that day, the answering machine light was blinking. He played the message. And then he called Kirk.

"We got a message," Tommy said. "Some guy named Sam Bartoniy wants to meet with us."

"From Bartoniy Rubbish Disposal?"

"I guess so."

"What about?"

"He didn't say. But he did say it will be worth our while. His office is over on North Avenue"

"No kidding … When does he want to meet?"

"This afternoon at four o'clock."

"Well, let's find out what he wants."

The Bartoniy Rubbish Disposal Inc. office was something out of the seventies, with its green shag rug, harvest gold appliances, and dark paneled walls. The air was pungent with cigarette smoke. A rotund middle-aged woman was sitting behind the reception desk when Tommy and Kirk entered. Smoke curled upward from a cigarette in the ashtray atop the desk.

"Can I help you boys?" the woman wheezed.

"We're here to see Mr. Bartoniy," Kirk told her.

"He expectin' you?"

"Yes ma'am. We're from Half Profit Recycling."

She picked up the phone and dialed. "Sam?"

"What!" barked a voice down the hall.

"There are two fellas here to see you. Say they're from a Half Profit something or other."

"Send them down Shirley!"

The receptionist pointed to a narrow, dimly-lit corridor. "Down the hall, first door on the left."

"Thanks ma'am."

The door to Sam Bartoniy's office was closed. Tommy knocked on it three times.

"Come in! Come in!"

Tommy opened the door and he and Kirk slowly entered the room. Sam Bartoniy was seated behind a huge desk with a chipped formica top. He looked up—and frowned. The man was obviously not expecting a pair of eighth graders. "You boys lost?"

"No sir."

"Is this some kind of joke?" he asked. "Or is your father on his way here?"

"...No."

"Your uncle then? An older brother perhaps? Who'd you boys come here with?"

"We didn't come here with anyone," said Tommy. "Half Profit Recycling is *our* business. Kirk and I are the owners."

Sam Bartoniy wrinkled his forehead..."Is that so?"

"Yes sir. We started it last fall."

Bartoniy's demeanor suddenly softened; his face creased in a slow grin. *This will be easy.*

"Is that right? Well, have a seat, boys. And tell me...just how old are you two?"

"Thirteen," said Kirk.

"Almost fourteen," Tommy put in.

"Thirteen! Hah! You two certainly are enterprising, I'll give you that. Boys, I'll cut to the chase. I was out on the route with one of my drivers this morning and I couldn't help noticing those green recycling barrels of yours around town. Mighty impressive for two thirteen-year-olds, I might add. But the problem is, you're interfering with my business, boys. You see, I was there first. And, well, business is business. You're cutting into my profits. But I'm not going to make a fuss over this. I'm a fair man. And I'm going to do you two a big favor. I'm going to buy your business—at a very competitive price."

The man pulled a contract from his desk drawer and placed it on the desktop. Then he scribbled something down on it. A few moments later he handed the contract to them.

"I'm giving you two hundred and fifty dollars—a good chunk of money for two eighth-graders, I might add. Just sign on the line and it's all yours. I'll get the cash." The man talked like it was a done deal. And then he stood up.

"Two hundred fifty dollars?" Kirk said.

"Yes. Like I said. That's a good sum of money for boys like yourselves. Think of the things you could buy with that kind of money!"

"The barrels alone are worth more than that," Tommy shot back.

Sam Bartoniy's face reddened. "Very well then, I'll double it. Five hundred dollars! I've got the cash in the safe. I'll be right back."

"No thanks," said Kirk.

"Are you boys nuts? Five hundred dollars isn't exactly pocket change."

"The business is worth more than five hundred dollars," Tommy pointed out. "A lot more."

"Oh, very well then. One thousand dollars. That's four times what I originally offered. And that's my final offer!"

Kirk and Tommy glanced at each other.

"No deal," said Kirk.

"That's right," Tommy confirmed. "Half Profit Recycling is not for sale."

"You boys are nuts turning down good money like that!"

"Maybe," said Tommy, as they got up to leave. "But that's our decision."

"You'll be sorry!" shouted Sam Bartoniy as they made their way down the hall. "You'll regret this. You're playing with the *big boys* now. Nobody refuses to do business with Sam Bartoniy!" The man meant it too. If he couldn't buy Half Profit Recycling, he'd force them out of business. And he knew just how to do it.

Chapter 17
An Unexpected Visitor

As a senior inspector with the Belton Inspectional Services Department, Jack Dilliche thought he had seen it all. He was familiar with practically every business in town, including all of the home-based businesses. Every time someone called in a complaint about one of the town's business establishments, it invariably ended up on his desk. That's exactly what happened when Sam Bartoniy called in with a complaint about Half Profit Recycling. Jack had seen a lot during his tenure…but this was a first: two middle school students running a business from a backyard shed.

At 3:45 in the afternoon the following day, Tommy was at the desk totaling receipts, and Kirk was reaching into the cooler for a pudding when they heard a knock on the shed's door.

They saw a tall man looking through the window. He appeared to be in his fifties. The guy wore dark slacks and white collared shirt with a brown tie. He had the height of an NBA player. In his hand was a clipboard. It had been weeks since they'd placed the ad, but they continued to get calls and occasional visits from job applicants.

"I think we have another job applicant outside," Kirk declared.

"They just keep coming."

"You want to break the news to him, or should I?" asked Kirk.

"Let's flip a coin."

The guy knocked again.

"We'll both tell him," Tommy said. He opened the door.

"Sorry, the position's been filled."

The man seemed surprised at first, but quickly regained his composure.

"*This is* Half Profit Recycling?" the man inquired.

"That's us," Tommy confirmed. "But like we said, the position is no longer available."

"Position?"

"You're here for the job we had advertised, right?" Tommy asked. "It's been filled. It's no longer available."

"On the contrary," the man replied, removing a pen from his pocket. "I'm not *looking* for a job. I *have* one. I'm Jack Dilliche… from Inspectional Services. I need to speak with the owners of Half Profit Recycling."

"I'm the owner," Tommy said. "One of them anyhow. And this is Kirk. He's the other owner. We're partners."

The man raised his eyebrows. "Well fellas," he said, "you're in violation of Code 7.3(a)."

Tommy and Kirk glanced at each other.

"Huh?"

"You're operating a business without a permit," the man explained. "The town mandates that every business must obtain a permit." He then removed a form from the clipboard and wrote something down on it.

"…Permit?" Kirk inquired.

"That's right. Don't worry. I'm just giving you a warning this time. You've got five business days to get down to town hall to apply for a permit. They cost twenty-five dollars." He handed them a warning slip.

"…Uh…we'll do that sir."

"Very well, boys. Good luck to you now."

With that, the man did an about face and headed back across the yard. Kirk glanced over at Tommy with a questioning look.

Tommy shrugged. "I guess we have to go legit."

Chapter 18
Enter The Press

Ana Goncalves, a senior reporter with *The Belton Times*, was at the town hall doing research. While there, she overheard a woman who worked in the Clerk's Office talking about two boys who came in to apply for a business permit. The woman was joking with a co-worker about how the two were only thirteen years-old. They had to have their parent's co-sign the permit application because they we under eighteen.

Ana found it amusing at first, nothing more…But when the woman mentioned the name of the business, it caught her attention. Like many of the town's residents, she lived in a Steibner building. She had been depositing her bottles and cans in the green recycling barrel that had recently been placed next to the dumpster—the barrel owned by Half Profit Recycling.

She never would have guessed the business was owned by a couple of thirteen year-olds. Ana Goncalves was always on the lookout for a good story. And this one seemed newsworthy.

Being the astute reporter that she was, it didn't take Ana Goncalves long to find the Atwill's home. The address was listed on Half Profit Recycling's business permit application. She knocked on the front door. Mrs. Atwill opened the door.

"Hi." Ana Goncalves extended her hand. "I'm a reporter with *The Belton Times*."

Mrs. Atwill hesitantly shook the woman's hand. "How can I help you, Miss Goncalves?"

"Actually, I'm here to talk to your son, Kirk, if he's a-round. And another boy—Tommy Hartwell."

"Is there a problem?" Mrs. Atwill inquired.

"Oh, no. It's nothing like that," the reporter assured her. "I'm interested in talking with them about their business. For a story. I think it would make a good one."

"Is that so? Well, they're out back." Mrs. Atwill motioned toward the back yard.

"Excellent. Thanks very much."

Were it not for the sign above the shed's door, Ana Goncalves never would have guessed it housed a business. She knock-ed on the door.

"Enter."

Ana Goncalves opened the door and peered inside …Her eyes widened.

The tiny room was bustling with activity. There were five people inside the room: a kid in his late teens lifting a bag of com-pressed cans; two kids sorting through a heap of cans; and two eighth-graders—one sitting behind a makeshift desk, totaling figures on a calculator, the other writing something down in a ledger book. All five of them stopped what they were doing and glanced up at the woman in the business suit.

"Kirk Atwill ? Tommy Hartwell?"

"That's us," declared Tommy. "I'm Tommy. And this is Kirk."

Ana Goncalves gave them a friendly smile. "Nice to meet you boys," she purred. "I'm a reporter for *The Belton Times.*"

Chapter 19
Facing Suspension

The article was published in the Monday edition of *The Belton Times.* Kirk's parents had just finished reading it when he stepped into the kitchen that morning.

"You and Tommy are front page news!" Mr. Atwill exclaimed. "Mighty impressive, son. You guy's are big time now. Way to go!"

"We sure are proud of you honey," said his mother, giving him a hug and a peck on the cheek. "It's a wonderful article. You two certainly deserve the praise Miss Goncalves has bestowed on you."

"Thanks Mom. Thanks Dad."

Kirk took a seat at the table. His father slid the paper over to him. The bold headline on the front page was hard to miss:

Two Local Eighth-graders Operate Booming Recycling Start-up Business

Kirk's heart thudded with excitement as he spread the paper out on the table and anxiously began to read...

Half Profit Recycling, a Belton-based start-up company, has rapidly expanded since beginning operations last fall. Half

Profit Recycling's dark green recycling barrels are a common sight around Belton now. You'll see them in each school, and you'll find them at each town-owned facility, from the library to the police department. But what you may not know is that this company is owned and operated by two local thirteen-year-olds. Two eighth-graders who attend Horace Clovis Middle School: Kirk Atwill and Tommy Hartwell...

The article went on about how Kirk and Tommy had always been entrepreneurial, how they would be out hauling rubbish while their friends were still asleep. Ana Goncalves touched on the business's humble beginnings as a project for the YOUNG ENTREPRENEURS CLUB, and how Kirk and Tommy donated half of each week's profits to charity.

The story carried over to the second page, where there was a picture of Kirk, Tommy, and Jeremy loading cans into Jeremy's truck. There was a second picture of them in front of the shed, the Half Profit Recycling Headquarters sign suspended overhead.

The phone rang just as Kirk finished the article.

"Chances are it's for you," his mother told him.

Kirk ambled over to the phone and picked it up. "Hello?"

"Did you read it!?" From his tone, Tommy was excited about the article too.

"Yep. Great article, eh?"

"Yeah, and the pictures came out pretty good too!"

"Sure did!"

"I'll bet the article will bring us even more business. Free advertising is what it is," said Tommy.

"For sure."

"Okay, catch you at school."

"Later."

From the stares and sideways glances they received in the hallway after first bell—from both students and teachers—it was apparent that people had either read the article or had heard about it. There seemed to be an excitement in the air. The word was out; their business was no longer a secret. Kids they didn't even know would stop their conversations, and look up at them as they passed by in the hall. The two of them had achieved a sort of instant celebrity status. It had all the makings of a banner day…but just across town was a completely different scene.

*****

Sam Bartoniy stomped into the office an hour later than usual thanks to a trip to the dentist office. The Novocain was wearing off. The pain from having two teeth extracted was starting to set in.

"Good morning," wheezed Shirley, as he stormed in past her desk without a word.

Shirley had left a copy of The Belton Times on his desk,

just like she did every Monday morning. And no sooner had he sat down than the headline on the front page caught his attention.

"What the—"

The man's face turned beet-red as he read the article.

"Those two delinquents are only thirteen years-old…"

Sam Bartoniy's demeanor suddenly changed; his frown gave way to a smile. "That's it! They're only thirteen—too young to work. The minimum working age is fourteen. I've got them now."

The article was a blessing. It was just the ammunition he needed to put Half Profit Recycling out of business once and for all. Sam Bartoniy wasted no time. He knew just what to do. All it would take was one phone call…to the mayor's office. Sam Barton picked up his phone and dialed…

Mayor Whitten was at his desk reading the article when his secretary forwarded the call through to him. He picked up the phone. "Mayor Whitten, how may I help you?" he asked.

"Mr. Mayor, this is Sam Bartoniy calling. Have you read the paper today?"

"As a matter of fact, I'm reading it right now."

"Interesting article on the front page about this so-called Half Profit Recycling outfit. I didn't know the town did business with kids—kids under fourteen years of age. Kids *under* the minimum working age."

"I'm as surprised as you are," the mayor told him. "And

I'm concerned too. We're going to get to the bottom of this right away; I can assure you of that. The matter will be thoroughly investigated."

Across town, Superintendent Stackner had just finished reading the article when the mayor called. "Yes sir," he told the mayor. "It was news to me as well, sir... I had no idea that Half Profit Recycling was run by students...I'm looking into it right now... This will be a top priority...Yes sir. I'll keep you updated."

After he hung up with the mayor, Superintendent Stackner called his secretary into his office.

"Marge, call Horace Clovis Middle School, and get Principal Philbrick on the horn."

"Right away, sir."

Marge stepped back into his office just minutes later. "I have Principal Philbrick on the line, sir. Shall I forward him to you?"

"Yes, by all means." The superintendent pushed the paper work on his desk aside and picked up the phone.

"Byron."

"Yes sir?"

"Have you read the paper today?"

The principal was at a loss. He didn't live in Belton. He didn't subscribe to *The Belton Times*.

"...Uh...No sir. I haven't."

The superintendent summarized the article. Philbrick's jaw dropped open as his boss brought him up to date.

"I knew those two were up to something!" blurted Philbrick.

"Sounds like you have a history with them."

"You might say that."

"Listen. We've got to address this, pronto," said the superintendent. "Do I make myself clear, Byron?"

"Yes sir. I'm on it sir."

"I hope so."

"I'll look into this right away, sir."

After he hung up, Principal Philbrick steamed out of the front office.

"Putnam!"

The janitor winced. He was waxing the gymnasium floor. It hadn't taken long for the principal to find him.

"Is it true!?" the principal asked.

"Is *what* true?"

"That this Half Profit Recycling outfit is owned by two students? Two eighth grade students from *our* school?"

"...Er...Yes...I thought you knew," the janitor replied.

"You thought I knew!?" Do you think I'd ever do business with students? Let them into the teacher's lounge? Allow them access to the school after school hours? It's preposterous!"

The principal tromped out of the gymnasium. Mr. Putnam went back to work.

A few minutes later, during homeroom, just before the

morning announcements, the school secretary's voice cackled over the loud the speaker.

"Attention please. Kirk Atwill and Tommy Hartwell. Please report to the front office."

Kirk gulped. All of the students in his homeroom looked over at him, as did the teacher. He caught up with Tommy in the hallway.

"What's up?" Kirk asked.

Tommy shrugged. "Don't know…but I'm guessing it's about the article." The two of them had been so excited about the article. They hadn't considered any consequences. Their secret was out.

They made their way down the hall toward the front office. Mr. Hardwick was in the copy room, just around the corner. He saw them headed his way.

"Boys," he called. Tommy and Kirk stopped and headed into the copy room.

"Congratulations! I read the article this morning. Why, I had no idea you two had brought your business so far! Good for you. I knew you two were going to do well—but I never would have guessed you would have been so successful so soon. Just amazing what you've done in so little time. Utterly amazing. I'm sure your parents are quite proud!"

"Thanks Mr. Hardwick."

"Stop by after school sometime. I'd enjoy hearing about your endeavors."

"We'll do that sir," said Kirk.

"You two make me proud."

They headed back to the hallway, the uneasy feeling in their stomachs temporarily softened from the conversation with their mentor. It returned soon enough though.

"Psssst!" The noise came from the janitor's closet. The door was cracked open. "Over here, boys."

Tommy and Kirk peered inside the janitor's closet, then stepped inside. Mr. Putnam closed the door behind them and turned on the light. "A word of caution boys," he warned. "Philbrick blew a fuse this morning. He knows that you two are behind the business. And he's pretty ticked."

Tommy and Kirk exchanged nervous glances.

"Thanks for the heads up, Mr. Putnam."

"Play it cool, boys. And good luck."

The door to the principal's office was closed when they arrived at the front office. "Have a seat over there," whispered Mrs. Tidwell, gesturing to a bench. But before they could sit down, the door to the principal's office opened.

"Enter gentlemen."

Kirk and Tommy cautiously stepped into the principal's office. The principal was seated behind his desk.

"Have a seat," he said, gesturing to the two small chairs before the desk. Kirk and Tommy sat down. The principal glared at them.

"I don't know who you thought you were fooling," he began. "But the joke's over. How you two thought you could con your way into doing business with this school and the other schools in the district, and the other town buildings, is beyond me. The game's over though. In fact, you're both facing suspension."

Kirk and Tommy gulped.

"Suspension?"

"That's right. *Suspension.* And it goes without saying that this business of yours has come to an end."

There was a pad of forms on top of his desk. Principal Philbrick ripped off the top sheet and scribbled something down. Then he removed another sheet and repeated the process. He handed them each a *NOTICE OF DISCIPLINARY HEARING.*

"Give these to your parents when you get home today. And have them sign them," he instructed. "Per the school district's administrative policy, students facing suspension are entitled to a hearing—before they're suspended. As you'll see in the notice, the hearing is scheduled for eight-thirty Wednesday morning. Two days from now. Your parents have a right to be present at this hearing. I need these forms signed and in my office by tomorrow morning at the start of school. Don't forget!"

"But Mr. Philbrick, my parents—"

"That will be all gentlemen," said the principal, cutting Tommy off before he had a chance to tell him that his parents were out of town.

"Um, my father—"

"I said that will be all," boomed Philbrick, cutting Kirk off this time. Kirk didn't get a chance to tell him that his father was out of town on a business trip. "You two can return to your homerooms now."

Everything they had worked so hard for was about to come to an end. And now they might even be suspended from school. A suspension could have long lasting ramifications. It would be a permanent blemish on their school record. A blemish that could very well carry over into high school. They guessed that it might even haunt them when they applied for college.

Back out in the hallway, Kirk sighed. "Any ideas?"

For once, Tommy was at a loss for words. "Not this time."

That night, Tommy asked his sister, Jenna, to sign the *NOTICE OF DISCIPLINARY HEARING*. And Jenna surprised him by signing it. She wrote her name on the line designated for *guardian*. She didn't even put up an argument. Something about the situation seemed to strike a nerve. She surprised Tommy once more when she told him she'd be at the hearing. In fact, she would drive him to school Wednesday morning. There was anger in her voice—and it wasn't directed at her brother.

Jenna had once attended a disciplinary hearing herself, back in middle school. She had always been a bit on the rebellious side, but the disciplinary hearing wasn't related to something she had done. On the contrary, she had been falsely accused of stealing money. The issue was with a girl whose locker was next to hers. This girl's mother had put ten dollars in her daughter's jacket pocket to bring to school for a field trip. The girl placed her jacket in her locker and forgot to bring the money to her homeroom that morning.

Jenna was at her locker later that morning when the girl came to get the money. Only the money wasn't there. The girl accused Jenna of stealing it. And a disciplinary hearing was scheduled. Toward the end of the hearing, it was discovered that the money was in an inside pocket in the girl's jacket. It had been there all along.

"Yeah, I'll be there," Jenna told Tommy.

Tommy was glad to have his sister on his side.

While Jenna actually seemed to be looking forward to the hearing, Mrs. Atwill was another story altogether. Though she certainly meant well, the woman was a worrier. Always had been. Mrs. Atwill was not a boisterous or argumentative person by nature. She did not enjoy confrontations. So, when Kirk broke the news about the disciplinary hearing, she was immediately worried. She had tried to reach Kirk's dad three times after hearing the news, but he was still manning the booth at a trade show out of town. He was out of town until Saturday. Not that they would have been any better off if Mr. Atwill was there. Like his wife, the man was easy going, never one to argue. But there's strength in numbers, and it would have been nice to have some extra support at the hearing.

Kirk's mother fretted over the situation during dinner that night. This only added to the heavy feeling in Kirk's stomach. Neither of them had much of an appetite. They just picked at the food on their plate. Indeed, there was good reason to worry.

Wednesday's used to be Kirk's favorite day of the week. Now he wished Wednesday would never arrive.

Chapter 20
Judgement Day

Wednesday morning. Kirk and his mother arrived at the front office at 8:20. Mrs. Atwill glanced around nervously. The school secretary offered her a coffee, but she kindly refused it. The woman was jittery enough as it was.

Tommy and Jenna arrived at 8:29AM. They had circled the block twice trying to find parking, but there were no spaces available. They ended up pulling into the faculty parking lot. A tall man in a pinstriped suit and dark wool overcoat was getting out of a Lincoln as they pulled in. The look on his face told them they were not allowed to park there. But of course they already knew that.

The door to the principal's office swung open promptly at 8:30 A.M. Principal Philbrick stepped out and said, "You may come in."

Kirk, Mrs. Atwill, Tommy, and Jenna entered the room single file. Principal Philbrick took a seat behind his desk. To his right sat the man in the pinstriped suit—Superintendent Stackner. Before the desk were four folding chairs.

The principal motioned to the chairs. "Sit down, please." He handed a clipboard to Mrs. Atwill. Attached to it was a sign-in sheet.

"Please sign in and pass this along."

As the sign-in sheet was being passed along the principal consulted with the superintendent. They spoke with hushed voices, but Kirk heard Superintendent Stackner say, "It's your school, Byron. *You* can get things started."

Philbrick nodded in anxious agreement. This was a big chance after all. His opportunity to show his stuff to his superior, make a good impression. Show him that he had what it took, that he was a take-charge administrator.

"Now then," Principal Philbrick said, clearing his voice. "Let us begin. As you all know, this is a disciplinary hearing. With me here today is Mr. Stackner, Superintendent of Belton Public Schools." The superintendent nodded, his face expressionless. Principal Philbrick opened a *Belton School District Students' Responsibilities and Rights Handbook*. He began to read page ten: "Students facing suspension—"

"Excuse me," blurted Jenna, cutting him off in mid-sentence. "You mentioned the word *suspension*. The hearing hasn't even been conducted yet, and you're implying that Tommy and Kirk are going to be suspended?"

An irritated look crossed the principal's face. The superintendent raised an eyebrow.

"And who are *you*?" asked Philbrick.

"Jenna Hartwell. I'm Tommy's sister—guardian."

Tommy and Kirk were sure glad to have her there. Jenna was a fighter. "Well, Miss Hartwell, the principal responded. "You'll notice I said *facing* suspension. These two haven't been suspended—*yet*. I was *about* to say, that students facing suspension are protected by the Fourteenth Amendment—the Due Process Clause of the Fourteenth Amendment that is. This means that these two students are afforded a hearing where they have a chance to tell their side of the story. Today, we are here for that hearing."

The superintendent nodded in agreement. Philbrick was quite pleased with himself. He hadn't had to refer to the handbook for that last part. The long hours of studying it over the past two days had paid off.

"So, let us begin," Philbrick said. "First of all, there are multiple issues here. A number of school rules have been broken—three in fact. First and foremost though, these two students, Tommy Hartwell and Kirk Atwill, have conned this school—all of the schools—into doing business with them. And they duped the town too, from what I hear—"

"Stop," said Jenna," cutting the man off once again.

The principal was dumbfounded. He hadn't counted on interruptions.

"You're accusing my brother and Kirk of something before you've heard their defence. It sounds like you've already made up your mind about the outcome of this so-called 'hearing.'" Tommy and Kirk glanced at one another.

Maybe things wouldn't turn out so bad after all, with Jenna there fighting for them.

Philbrick's face reddened. He was ready to blow. "Young lady— "

Superintendent Stackner put his hand on the principal's shoulder. "I'll handle this, Byron," he said in his calm manner. He saw where this was going. The man had attended too many meetings and hearings that rambled on needlessly because of interruptions. It only took one person to steer you off course, he knew.

"Miss Hartwell, you look to be of high school age, am I correct? A junior, or senior perhaps?"

"That's right," beamed Jenna. "I'm a senior."

"And you go to Belton High?"

"Yes, I do."

"I see…And do you have written permission to be missing school at this time?"

"…Well…no, but I— "

"Then I suggest you be on your way," the superintendent instructed. "Skipping school is not something the school district takes lightly. In fact, it could bar you from participating in certain school activities… such as the Prom, for example.

Jenna's face suddenly paled. "Um…yes sir."

Kirk and Tommy slumped as Jenna stood up. When Jenna left, so too did their hopes. It came down to Mrs. Atwill now. She was their only hope. Unfortunately, it just wasn't her nature to be vocal. But she surprised them.

"I expect that Kirk and Tommy *will* get a chance to tell their side of the story?" she asked, is as stern a voice as she could muster.

"That's right," acknowledged the superintendent. "They

will. But we need to follow protocol here. Per school policy, Principal Philbrick first needs to cite the rules that were allegedly broken—the alleged infractions."

"Very well," she replied. It was not looking good. And to make matters worse, the school secretary knocked on the door and announced a latecomer…Mayor Whitten.

"Sorry I'm late," said the mayor, pulling up a chair beside Superintendent Stackner, just as Jenna left the room "Please continue. Don't let me interrupt."

Kirk and Tommy, wishing they were anywhere but where they were, wished they could disappear.

"Welcome, Mayor Whitten," said Principal Philbrick. "I was just about to announce the three school rules that have been broken by Mr. Atwill and Mr. Hartwell. But, before I do, it's important to note that, unlike lesser infractions, each of these infractions is grounds for suspension—up to a week's suspension per infraction. What's more, because three separate rules may have been broken, *expulsion* is not out of the question.

Mrs. Atwill jumped in her seat. Kirk's jaw dropped open. Tommy's face paled. Suspension was bad enough. And it was a given that they would loose the business. Philbrick had already said as much. But *expulsion*? Expulsion was something altogether different. They hadn't considered this.

Superintendent Stackner put his hand on Philbrick's shoulder again and whispered into his ear. Philbrick nodded. "Okay, maybe expulsion is a bit harsh," he said. "But *suspension* is not. Now then, the three infractions are as follows: *Lying To*

School Officials. Being In An Unauthorized Area. And
Unauthorized Use of School Property."

"We'll begin with the first one: *Lying To School
Officials.*"

Kirk's mom stood up. "Excuse me, Principal Philbrick.
Kirk and Tommy don't lie. They're good boys. Hardworking
and—"

"With all due respect Mrs. Atwill, they most certainly did
lie. It's very clear that they lied their way into doing business with
this school and the other schools in the district. And perhaps they
used the same tactics to win business with other town facilities too.
They obviously lied about their age. The school district doesn't do
business with *kids*."

The superintendent did not comment, just took it all in.

"And I'm sure the town doesn't make a practice of doing
business with kids either," Philbrick added.

The mayor nodded.

Philbrick was pleased with himself. He liked the way
things were going. "Doing business with a couple of eighth-
graders is…it's…well, it's unthinkable. Out of the question. And
it's quite obvious these two lied to get their foot in the door and
place their so-called recycling barrels in the schools. "

"We didn't—"

The superintendent stood up and cut Tommy off. "You'll
have a chance to speak, son. Both of you will. But first, we need to
let Principal Philbrick finish. Continue, Byron."

"Lying is just the first infraction though," Philbrick went

on. "The second infraction—*Being In An Unauthorized Area*—is also very much a concern. It's quite obvious that this rule too has been broken. Students are not permitted in the schools after school hours and on weekends without permission, unless it's for special school sponsored events. And there's the teacher's lounges too. These are strictly off limits to students, but you two have been in every teacher's lounge in the school district. And that brings us to the third infraction: *Unauthorized Use of School Property*—"

Just then door the creaked open. Mrs. Tidwell poked her head into the room.

"Excuse me, sir, but there's someone else here for the hearing."

Mr. Hardwick stepped into the room. He'd caught wind of the hearing earlier that morning when he overheard the school secretary talking to one of the teachers about it in the front office. He had been listening just outside the room.

"I've been listening to this hearing for a while, Byron," he said. "As far as I can tell, Kirk and Tommy haven't had a chance to tell their side of the story yet. Everything seems a little one-sided so far." Tommy and Kirk were suddenly infused with a surge of hope. Why hadn't they thought to consult Mr. Hardwick about this before?

"Listen, Mr. Hardwick, this is a disciplinary hearing. It's a private matter. These hearings are not open to the public. I'm going to have to ask you to leave the room. You don't have a right to be here."

"Actually Byron, I think I *do* have a right to be here. I may be partly responsible for Kirk and Tommy being here in the first place. I'd like to represent Kirk and Tommy if they'll allow me the honor."

"Out of the question," barked Philbrick. "These two are here because of their own actions, not yours."

Mr. Hardwick reached into his briefcase and held up a copy of the *Belton School District Students' Responsibilities and Rights Handbook*. "You'll see on page twelve, paragraph three, that students facing suspension are 'entitled to representation, at their own expense.'"

"We're too far along now—"

Superintendent Stackner put his hand on Philbrick's shoulder yet again and leaned in to talk to him. The mayor joined in. The three of them broke into a hushed conversation. They perused page twelve of the *Belton School District Students' Responsibilities and Rights Handbook* at Philbrick's desk.

As the three men talked, Kirk, Tommy, and Mrs. Atwill turned toward Mr. Hardwick. He gave them a thumbs up and smiled.

The superintendent turned his attention to Tommy and Kirk a few moments later. "Gentlemen, is it your wish to have Mr. Hardwick represent you?"

"Yes sir!" they agreed in unison.

"And it's okay with you, Mrs. Atwill?"

"Oh yes. Yes it is."

"Very well then. Mr. Hardwick, you may stay and represent Kirk and Tommy. I guess now would be as good a time as any to reconvene. You have the floor."

"Thanks very much," Mr. Hardwick began, stepping forward into the room. "Every story has two sides. And I think it's time we heard from Tommy and Kirk. I must say too, that I don't think we'll be here long. I don't have many questions for Kirk and Tommy, both of whom are former pupils of mine—and great students I might add."

Philbrick frowned. He had never cared much for Hardwick. The two of them had never seen eye-to-eye.

"I understand you boys have two recycling barrels in the school cafeteria here at Horace Clovis Middle School," Mr. Hardwick began. "And another one in the teacher's lounge—three in all. Is that correct?"

"That's right," Tommy confirmed.

"And do you have permission to have the barrels in these locations?"

"Yes," said Kirk.

Tommy nodded in agreement. "That's right."

"And *who* gave you permission?"

"…Uh…Mr. Putnam, the janitor."

Philbrick shot up from his chair. "Mr. Putnam is not authorized to give permission!"

Superintendent Stackner frowned. "It's their turn now, Byron. Let them have their say."

The principal returned to his seat.

"All right," Mr. Hardwick continued, focusing his attention on Kirk and Tommy. "Your business, Half Profit

Recycling, has recycling barrels at the other schools too, correct?"

"That's right," Kirk and Tommy replied in unison.

"Now, about *those* recycling barrels. Did you ask the janitors at the other schools for permission to place them there as well?"

"Uh, no. It wasn't like that," said Tommy. "We didn't ask for the business…It kind of came to us."

"Oh? Please explain."

"We got a phone call," Tommy explained.

"A phone call you say? From whom?"

Tommy hunched his shoulders and looked at the floor. " Um…from Superintendent Stackner."

Mr. Hardwick's eyebrows shot up. "Superintendent Stackner called Half Profit Recycling?"

"Yes sir."

The tables were suddenly turned. Mr. Hardwick looked over at the superintendent. The man nodded and said, "I saw the recycling barrels here at Horace Clovis Middle School and as- sumed the business was legitimate. I thought all of the schools would do well to have recycling barrels—I still do."

"Did you inquire about their age?"

Superintendant Stackner paused for a moment. Then he shook his head no. "I didn't actually *talk* to anyone. I left a mes- sage on Half Profit Recycling's answering machine. My secretary is the one who actually spoke to them."

"So they didn't *lie* to you about their age—or anything else?"

"No. They did not."

Mr. Hardwick shot a glance at Principal Philbrick. "Well, that certainly puts things under a different light, doesn't it? And it proves that the first alleged infraction is not valid. Kirk and Tommy did not *lie* to a school official."

Principal Philbrick's shoulders sagged.

Mr. Hardwick forged on.

"Now, about the other two *infractions* these boys are accused of — *Being In An Unauthorized Area* and *Unauthorized Use of School Property*. From what I've just heard, Kirk and Tommy here *were* authorized to be in each of the schools, and they *were* authorized to use school property."

Superintendent Stackner cleared his throat. "Thank you, Mr. Hardwick. You've certainly shed some light on these matters. Do you have anything else to add?"

Mr. Hardwick smiled. "As a matter of fact, yes. I do have one final question for these boys."

"Please continue."

Mr. Hardwick shifted his focus back to Kirk and Tommy. "Tell me, why did you name your business *Half Profit Recycling*?"

"It was actually Tommy's idea," Kirk said. "It's because we give half of our profits to charity."

"You give *half* of the money you make to charity?"

"Yes sir," Kirk confirmed. "We've been donating half our profits to the thrift shop downtown. The thrift shop is a nonprofit. All of their proceeds go to helping people in need."

The superintendent's eyebrows lifted. So did the mayor's.

"Bravo boys!" praised Mr. Hardwick. "I have no more questions. You two have set a fine example for us all."

"Okay folks," said the superintendent. "Time for a ten-minute break."

Kirk, Tommy, and Mrs. Atwill followed Mr. Hardwick out into the front office. Kirk and Tommy weren't out of the woods yet, but things sure were looking a lot better. They thanked Mr. Hardwick profusely. He said it was nothing at all, told them he felt responsible after all, where the business was created in his class-room.

Ten minutes later everyone was back in the principal's office. "Well, we have some good news… and some bad news," the superintendent began. "The good news is… Tommy and Kirk will not be suspended."

Mrs. Atwill breathed a sigh of relief. Mr. Hardwick smiled. Kirk and Tommy grinned.

"And," the superintendent continued, directing his attention to Kirk and Tommy, "you two are to be commended for your donations to charity and for your thoughtfulness. It is truly remarkable. Like Mr. Hardwick said, this can be as lesson to us all." The superintendent meant it too. He had been pulling for Kirk and Tommy the whole time. He'd had a boyhood business with a friend. They sold used tools door-to-door.

"But now for the bad news—"

The mayor suddenly stood up. "I'd like to handle this part

if I may," he cut in. All eyes shifted to the mayor.

"Indeed, it's quite commendable how you two have donated half of your profits to charity," the major began. "It is truly admirable. And you've done a good thing for the environment as well, I might add. But the bad news that Superintendent Stackner was about to break to you involves the town as well as the schools. The bad news is…that neither the town nor the schools can continue to do business with Half Profit Recycling the way it is currently structured."

The emotional roller coaster that Kirk and Tommy had been on plunged downward once again.

"The reason," the mayor explained, "is that the minimum working age in this country is fourteen. We did some research made some calls. It's all quite clearly outlined by The US Department of Labor. Employers can not employ someone less than fourteen years of age. You boys are too young."

Tommy and Kirk sighed. It had been a good ride. And now it was over. Mrs. Atwill gave them each a sympathetic pat on the shoulder. And then Mr. Hardwick stood up.

"You're right, Mayor Whitten," he said. "The minimum working age is fourteen. And an employer can not hire someone who is under fourteen years of age…but Kirk and Tommy are not *employees* of the school district or the town. The school district and the town do not *pay* them. Furthermore, their business, Half Profit Recycling, does not charge a fee for its services. And I'd like to add, that Half Profit Recycling is a registered business, just like their competitor, Bartoniy Rubbish Disposal Inc. Bartoniy

Rubbish Disposal Inc. does business with the schools and the town, but the owner of that business and his staff are not *employees* of the schools or the town. And neither are Tommy and Kirk. If they were employees, they'd be on the payroll. But they're not."

Silence. The mayor, the superintendent and the principal seemed to be processing this information. The three of them moved to the back of the room and huddled together. They talked quietly. Minutes ticked by like hours. Finally, they turned around and faced the others.

"Well, we've talked things over a bit," the mayor stated. "You've raised some interesting points, Mr. Hardwick. We're going to need to run this by the town's legal counsel. And the school district will likely need to review this with the school committee. But if everything works out, Half Profit Recycling can continue to do business with both the schools and the town."

The look on Kirk and Tommy's faces was one of astonishment. They had braced themselves for the worst. And now, as they registered the possibility that they might not loose their business after all, they couldn't help but smile.

Brriiiiinngg!

First period had come to an end. And so had the disciplinary hearing.

Chapter 21
Middle School Millionaires

Three weeks after the disciplinary hearing, the town's legal counsel and the school committee found no wrongdoing. Half Profit Recycling was allowed to stay in business and continue operations. There was a requirement for the business to obtain insurance. Tommy's father helped obtain this. And Kirk and Tommy's parents had to sign some forms on their behalf, where they were minors. But that was it.

When Ana Goncalves caught wind of the disciplinary hearing and its positive outcome, she wrote another article. Then the phone started to ring. Business prospered in the weeks that followed. It seemed people were genuinely intrigued by a business run by two thirteen-year-olds.

The first call was from the textile mill. They wanted a barrel for their employee lunchroom. Then, Belton Wash-O-Matic asked for one too. The community college called, as did Belton Bowlarama and a number of other area businesses. And surprisingly, Principal Philbrick referred some business to them—his brother managed a manufacturing plant that needed a recycling barrel in its break room.

Over the next few months, Half Profit Recycling added more than two dozen new accounts. And Tommy, Kirk, Jeremy and the others on the Half Profit Recycling team worked harder than ever.

On the second Thursday in June, Kirk and Tommy were in the shed after school. Jeremy was out collecting; the five other kids they now had working for them were outside sorting bottles and cans. Tommy was at the desk reconciling their checking account... He whistled.

Kirk was reaching to the cooler for a Coke. He looked over at his partner.

"We're *millionaires*," Tommy declared, a big grin on his face.

"Funny." It certainly wasn't the first time Tommy had joked around. Kirk knew they were doing well, but they'd need thousands of accounts to become millionaires. That day was a long, long way off.

"I'm not kidding," Tommy said.

"Yeah, right."

"We're millionaires," Tommy repeated. His face grew serious. "We have ten thousand dollars in the account—a million pennies!"

Kirk smiled. "Penny millionaires. I like it." Their business had reached a milestone.

What the two of them didn't know at the time was that they *were* on their way to becoming actual millionaires. Half Profit Recycling prospered in the years that followed. By their senior year in high school, Half Profit Recycling had expanded into three more towns. Kirk and Tommy owned four trucks. By the time they graduated from high school they were making more money than their parents.

Kirk and Tommy kept at the business through their college years. Both of them majored in business administration. And in some of their classes, they found they actually knew more about the subject matter than their professors.

Their big coup came just after college graduation. Using what they had learned in college, they went national and franchised their business. Three years later, there were Half Profit Recycling franchise businesses operating in each of the bottle bill states. Kirk and Tommy were millionaires by age twenty-six. They were set for life.

And they didn't forget about those who had helped them along the way. Jeremy, who had stayed on from the start, was promoted to chief operating officer. Mr. Hardwick took early retirement from the school system and came onboard as controller. Mr. Putnam, after years of manual labor, took a desk job as director of operations. Tommy's sister, Jenna, was the office manager. And Tommy's grandmother helped out in the office from time to time.

Half Profit Recycling continued to order barrels from Jacob's Hardware, though it was Mr. Jacob's son they did business with now. Mr. Jacob retired to Florida, thanks largely to the high volume of barrels the store sold.

They continued to donate half of their profits to charity. They still donated to the thrift store, but there were many other charities they donated to as well, ultimately helping thousands of people in need.

And as big as their business was, it continued to grow. Half Profit Recycling diversified and entered the rubbish disposal businesses in the years that followed. And they bought their old competitor, Bartoniy Rubbish Disposal Inc.

Though they could have lived anywhere they chose, Kirk and Tommy continued to reside in Belton. And they gave something back to the community. Something in addition to all of the money they donated to charity. They both volunteered their time as instructors for The YOUNG ENTREPRENEURS CLUB, where they passed along the most valuable business advice they ever received: *Sometimes, the best way to make money is to give it away.*

Made in the USA
Middletown, DE
15 December 2016